Hiding Out

Peter was having so much fun exploring the cave that he didn't notice what the rest of the family were doing, so when the car started up he had a terrible shock. Had his parents really driven off without him and left him alone in the French countryside? Not sure what to do for the best, Peter decides to hide out and wait for his parents to come back, but surviving in a strange country is not an easy matter and Peter has to rally all his resources to stay alive.

An exciting and intriguing story from popular author Elizabeth Laird.

Other books by Elizabeth Laird

Red Sky in the Morning – *Macmillan*

Kiss the Dust – *Egmont*

Jay – *Egmont*

Forbidden Ground – *Puffin*

Jake's Tower – *Macmillan*

The Garbage King – *Macmillan*

A Little Bit of Ground – *Macmillan*

Paradise End – *Macmillan*

Secrets of the Fearless – *Macmillan*

Wild Things (series) – *Macmillan*

Elizabeth Laird

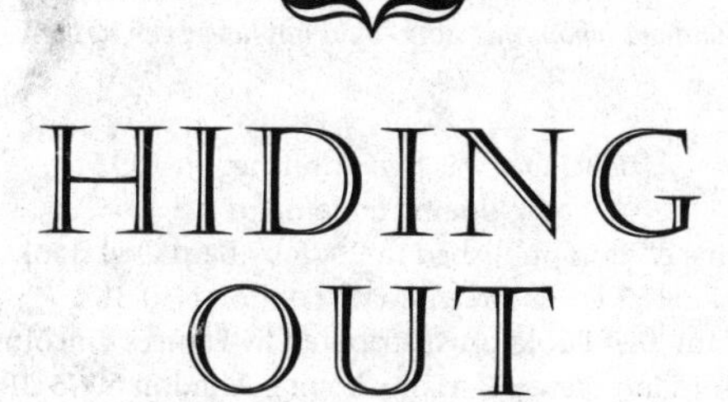

HIDING OUT

BA[illegible]S

For Angela and Bernard
and all at Châtelperron.

My grateful thanks are due to William McDowall,
without whom this story could not have been written

Hiding Out was first published in 1993
by William Heinemann Ltd
This edition published in 2006 by Barn Owl Books
157 Fortis Green Road, London N10 3LX
Barn Owl Books are distributed by Frances Lincoln
4 Torriano Mews, Torriano Avenue, London NW5 2RZ

ISBN 1-903015-53-6

Designed and typeset by Douglas Martin
Printed and bound in China for Imago

Barn Owl Books gratefully acknowledges
the financial assistance of Arts Council England
in this publication

{1}

It was cool in the cave. Peter Castle stood just inside the entrance and peered in. He could still feel the sun beating down, uncomfortably hot on his back, while wafts of fresh, earth-smelling air washed over his face from the silence and darkness within.

He looked over his shoulder to check that the others hadn't seen him. His sister Rachel was paddling in the stream, on the other side of a narrow field. Julian and Sophie Fletcher were squabbling over the early blackberries that dotted the hedgerow. The grown-ups were still lolling about in the long grass beneath the thick fringe of willows and hazels that shaded the stream. Around them were strewn the remains of the picnic. The heat seemed to have made them sleepy. They were no longer bothering to beat at the wasps and flies that clustered round the peach stones and melon rinds on their abandoned plates.

Everyone had gathered round the cave mouth when they had first driven up in their cars. Peter had wanted to go in and look round there and then, but Dad had pointed to a notice half hidden under a tangle of brambles: *Interdit au Public. Danger.*

"Better not, Pete. Might be hungry cavemen lurking about in there."

Peter hadn't answered. When Dad treated him (as he constantly did) as if he was still ten or eleven years old, as if he still played 'let's pretend' games and collected football stickers, Peter tried to ignore him.

Billie Fletcher had answered him though. She was even more stupid than her children.

"Oh, honestly, Tom. You're giving me the creeps. Again."

"Silly Billie," Dad had said fatuously. "You'd love to meet a caveman. He'd grab you by the hair and drag you into his cave and . . ."

Billie had squealed. Peter's mother had suddenly become interested in a butterfly sunning itself on the notice, and had pointed it out to Rachel.

Peter took another step into the cave. It was bigger than it looked from the outside. You had to duck your head at the entrance in order to get in, but inside the roof was arched so that it was quite easy to stand up.

The midday glare had been so fierce that for a moment the cave seemed completely dark. Then Peter saw a glimmer of light some way ahead. Gingerly, he felt his way towards it, running his hands along the pale, crumbling surface of the wall. Underfoot the uneven floor of rock, with soft pockets of fine dusty sand, sloped gradually upwards.

His eyes were adjusting now. He could see the whole cave. It wasn't very large, no bigger than the Castles' sitting-room at home, although it was only possible to stand up straight in the middle, as the rounded roof sloped down on all sides, like an attic room.

Peter could see the source of the green light now. It came from a shaft in the rock, just wide enough to wriggle through (if you could find hand and footholds in the soft earth of the sides) which must lead out into the field above. The green colour was caused by a filter of leaves and tufts of grass that grew out of the funnel walls.

A back door, thought Peter. That's handy. I could live here. I'd light the fire over there, near the entrance, and I could sit on that boulder beside it, and make a bed with bracken or something, and keep my things in that little hole in the wall.

"Peter!" Rachel was calling him. Her voice, coming from the field outside, sounded strangely dead and muffled at the back of the cave. "Come on, Peter! We're going to dam the stream. We need you!"

Peter went back to the entrance. He could move around easily in the cave now that his eyes were used to the dimness. He peered out, shielding his body from view behind an elder bush which grew by the mouth of the cave.

Rachel had her back to him, and was running away towards the stream, her bright yellow shorts bobbing about like a giant butterfly as she zigzagged across the rough grass, trying to avoid the clumps of thistle.

"Can't find him!" she called to Sophie, who had stopped blackberrying and was peeling off her socks, ready to paddle too. "He must have gone off somewhere with Julian."

Peter let his breath out. He was safe from the girls, anyway.

If I lived here, I'd make it more private, he thought. Build a wall across the front, with twigs and stuff, and weave a proper door out of bark and sticks that could actually swing back.

There was a picture of a door like that in his survival handbook, in the section on shelters. He'd studied it (and all the other diagrams) time and again. This cave would be a gift to a plane crash survivor, or a soldier in enemy territory, or a runaway prisoner, or the last person left alive at the end of World War Three.

There were a few sticks lying on the cave floor. Peter picked one up. It was so old and rotten it snapped in his fingers. No one could weave with that. A dead stem of old man's beard that was hanging down above the entrance looked more promising. Peter bent it between his fingers. It felt springy and strong.

I need my Swiss army knife to cut this, he thought. He saw a snapshot of the knife in his mind's eye. He knew exactly where it was: under the driver's seat in the car beside his mobile phone. He'd been pushing them backwards and forwards with the toe of his shoe all morning, to relieve the boredom of the awful journey from the holiday cottage in the Dordogne to Calais and the Channel ferry.

Cautiously, he slipped out of the cave and looked round. Down by the stream, Billie Fletcher was lying on the grass. Her T-shirt had parted from her coral pink skirt, exposing a paler pink expanse of midriff. She and Dad were both roaring with laughter. Mum was packing up the picnic, snapping the lids down on the plastic containers of salad and half-eaten cheeses, and shaking the table-cloth hard. Julian was the danger. He'd followed Peter about for the entire holiday, watching, spying, giving away every secret place, spoiling every private moment. Of all people, Peter didn't want Julian in his cave.

The two cars, the Fletchers' and the Castles' own, were pulled up near the gate leading into the field a little further along the lane. Peter sauntered across to them, trying to look casual. If Julian popped out from somewhere he could pretend he was fetching a book, and say he was going to look for somewhere quiet to read. Nothing irritated Julian more. He never read anything. He told anyone who'd listen that books were practically obsolete in the computer age, anyway.

Peter reached the car. No one had seen him. He felt around in the mass of luggage piled up behind the back seat. He found the knife, and on an impulse, he picked up his anorak too. Bundled up, it would be comfortable to sit on while he did his weaving. He'd have another hour, with luck, before the grown-ups were ready to move off again. Plenty of time to make his woven door.

{2}

A dragonfly whisked past Rachel's nose, almost grazing her with its luminous blue wings. She'd been bending over in the bed of the stream, but she stood up, a dripping stone in her hands, to watch it settle on a rock that stuck out of the wet mud of a miniature beach on the outer edge of a bend in the stream. Something that looked like a pine cone next to it wriggled, and made a clumsy leap into the water.

A frog, thought Rachel. She was fond of frogs. That was what she liked best about the country in France. There were a lot more things like frogs and voles and red squirrels about than there were at home. She never saw anything exciting from nature in her own garden.

The dam was coming along quite well. She wedged her stone on top of the pile that she and Sophie had collected already. The flow of water had reduced itself down to a trickle at this side of the stream, and was rushing through on the far side with satisfactory sucking and gurgling noises which mostly covered up the grown-ups' cross voices.

Mrs Castle suddenly appeared where the trees and bushes formed a gap above the little beach.

"Time to go, girls. Put your socks and shoes on."

"Mum! We've only just . . ."

"You heard me, Rachel."

"But why can't we . . .?"

"That's *enough.*"

Rachel could see that there was no point in arguing.

"Me and Sophie want to go in our car. Can we, Mum? Please?"

"I couldn't care less what you do. I just want to get going *now.*"

Regretfully, the girls waded out of the stream. Their little dam held bravely.

"Perhaps it'll still be here next year if we come back," said Sophie.

"Yeah, perhaps." Rachel looked up at her mother who was collecting up the last few scraps of litter. "Where's Dad?"

"Loading up the picnic things. He's going with Billie. I'm driving our car."

"Oh!" Rachel was surprised. Dad usually tried to prevent Mum driving, especially abroad. He usually insisted on driving his own car himself.

The girls forced their still wet feet into their canvas shoes, picked up their socks and followed Mrs Castle across the field. Mr Castle was already sitting in the driving seat of Billie's car. Billie herself was in the passenger seat, turning round to talk to Julian in the back.

"Where's Peter?" said Mrs Castle.

"He was with Julian," said Rachel.

Mr Castle started Billie's car and began to reverse out of the entrance to the field where she'd parked it. Rachel heard Billie say something, and her father guffaw in reply.

"Have you got Peter?" Mrs Castle shouted furiously, as Billie's car began to bump noisily down the rutted lane. Mr Castle looked down at the petrol gauge. It showed 'half-full'. He poked his head out of the window.

"Yes, it's okay. See you at Calais."

Mrs Castle jumped into the driving seat, reversed into the gate post, swore, clashed the car into first gear, let out the clutch too soon and set off in pursuit. Rachel and Sophie were jerked backwards. They looked at each other for a moment, wondering whether it was funny or not, and then burst out laughing. Rachel put her hands up to start their favourite clapping game.

"My boyfriend's name is Fatty,
He comes from Cincinatti . . ."

Mrs Castle said, over her shoulder, "Can't you do that more quietly, girls? I've got a splitting headache."

"Sorry, Mum."

They began again in whispers.

"How's your mother? All right.
Died in the fish shop, last night.
What did she die of? Raw fish.
How did she die? Like this!"

They banged their heads together.

"Ow! Watch it, Soph. That hurt!"

"Sorry."

They'd already turned out of the farm lane onto the main road for Paris and Calais.

{3}

Sitting in the cave on a convenient boulder, just beside the spot where he would have had his fireplace if he'd been a caveman, Peter vaguely heard the other's voices approaching and the doors of the two cars opening and slamming shut. Regretfully, he stood up, closed his knife and looked out. Julian was getting into the back seat of the Fletchers' car, and Dad and Billie were packing things into the boot.

He drew back out of sight. If the girls were going with Mum, they'd expect him to go with Julian. He'd have to sit in the same car as Dad and Billie, fending off Julian, who'd be whining on and on about his favourite computer game.

It looked as if Dad would drive off first. He'd wait till they'd gone, then hop into the front seat of their own car, beside Mum.

He turned back into the cave to fetch his things, and picked up the bit of weaving he had already done. He might as well take it with him. It would remind him of this cave. His cave. This past hour had been the best part of this whole awful holiday.

He stepped outside, his hands full of his things, in time to see his mother jump into her car and start off down the lane. For a moment, he stood still, too shocked to act. Then he dropped everything, and ran forward.

"Mum! Stop! Mum!"

Incredibly, she didn't hear him. The car gained speed. He ran after it, expecting it to stop. It didn't. He was running in dead earnest now, faster than he'd ever run in his life. For a moment he thought he could catch the car up. The gap was closing. He even heard, floating out of the back window, *"My boyfriend's name is Fatty, He comes from . . ."*

"Mum!" he shrieked again. But the wheels were rumbling and rolling noisily over the loose surface of the lane, and the car was speeding up. It was racing further and further away. Then it turned a corner, and was out of sight.

Peter's breath was coming in painful heaves. He willed his legs to make a last spurt, but they refused. It would be stupid, in any case, to go on running. He'd never catch them now. He slowed to a trot, then to a walk, and then he stopped altogether

My mobile! he thought. Where is it? Then he remembered. It was under the seat in the car, where he'd left it.

There was suddenly, all round him, an appalling silence. The only sounds were Peter's sobbing gasps for breath.

"They've gone! They've left me behind!" he said out loud, but the idea was incredible. He couldn't take it in.

I'm all on my own, he thought. In the middle of France. I don't even know the name of this place. I don't know where I am.

Before he knew what he was doing he'd started to run again, hopelessly pursuing the car, but a stitch in his side jogged him, and he stopped. He was suddenly blinded by tears.

It's all the Fletchers' fault, he thought. They've wrecked everything. I hate them!

He felt so angry he threw his head back and shouted, "I hate you!"

A blackbird squawked in fright, and shot out of a thorn bush nearby. Something rustled behind him. He turned. A sheep had got out of its field. It was standing up to its shoulders in the thick grass of the ditch between the edge of the lane and the hedge. It stopped chewing when Peter looked at it and stood quite still, staring at him.

Peter took a step towards it. The sheep reared its head, scrambled out of the ditch with a lumbering jump and trotted off. Somehow, the sight of its dirty, woolly bottom bobbing up and down was comforting. It must be going somewhere. There must be somewhere for it to go. There must be a farm near here, with people. Perhaps there was a village, with telephones, and even a policeman. They must be doing whatever they normally did on a Saturday afternoon.

His brain had started working now. He was able to think. They'll find I'm not with them when they get to Calais, or before then if they have to stop for petrol. They'll come back for me. All I've got to do is wait.

He nearly sat down then and there beside the road.

Then he remembered his anorak and his book.

I'll go back to my cave and wait there, he thought.

He felt a slight sense of relief. His stitch had gone. He'd got his breath back. Now he was only boiling hot from running in the sun. It would be cool in the cave. It wouldn't be too bad, waiting there.

The lane wound between high, thick hedgerows at the bottom of a small rise, which was covered with scrubby undergrowth. Above it were fields where the sheep were clustered under a clump of old oak trees, keeping themselves out of the sun. On the other side of the lane, cows grazed in the lusher meadows, watered by the stream on the far side, beyond which rose a rounded hill.

Peter looked at it all properly for the first time. Before, when they'd only stopped here for a picnic, he'd had no sense that this valley was a real place. Except for the cave, which he'd recognised at once as his own, it had made no more impression on him than a motor-way service station. It only seemed to exist while you were in it.

It was all here before we came, he thought. It was, somehow, an extraordinary thought.

He found his things where he'd dropped them, at the mouth of the cave. He picked them up and went inside.

{4}

The cave looked exactly the same as it had done a short while earlier, and yet something was different. It seemed wilder, and more real.

It's the silence, thought Peter. While the others had been picnicking nearby, a background of voices and laughter had somehow tamed the cave. It had been like being in the house with all the windows open when everyone else was in the garden. It was not at all like that now. The only sounds were the faint rustling of the wind in the dry leaves of the hedge, and the distant gurgling of the stream.

Might as well go on weaving, I suppose, thought Peter. Got to do something to pass the time.He picked up his knife and began hacking at a piece of old man's beard. The knife slipped, and nearly cut him. Peter shut it, and put it back in his pocket. Somehow, the woven door was no longer fun. It belonged to a game, to a pretence that the cave was a house. He wasn't in the mood for games any more.

He sat down on the boulder where he'd sat before to try to work things out.

They usually stop for petrol and things every three hours or so, he thought. Pity they filled up before we left the main road. It'll be at least two hours before they need to stop again. Then they've got to come back, which makes it four hours at least.

Four hours! His heart sank. He looked at his watch. It was three now. It would be at least seven o'clock before he could expect them. By then it would be getting dark.

Then Peter thought of something else, and his stomach lurched uncomfortably.

They wouldn't know where to find him! They'd never found out the name of this place. Dad had just taken a likely looking turning off the main road, and driven until he'd found a stream and a good place to picnic. They hadn't even looked it up on the map. It would be almost impossible in the half-darkness to find it again.

He stood up and took a step towards the mouth of the cave, then turned back. He felt paralysed. He had no idea what to do.

I suppose I'd better find a farm, and tell someone I'm here, he thought. They'd get in touch with the police or something.

He felt scared at the idea of trying to explain what had happened in French.

"Ma mère et mon père," he said, trying it out in his head, and paused. *"Et ma soeur,"* he added. He tried hard to visualize the pages of his French text book, but he couldn't produce the words for 'go', or 'leave behind', or 'lost'. He'd never bothered much with French at school. He'd only ever properly learned Unit 1.

"Bonjour. Je m'appelle Pierre. J'habite à Croydon."

The silence was suddenly broken by a new sound. A

vehicle was coming up the lane. Peter's heart bounded with joy.

"They've come back!" he shouted. He began to run along the lane to meet them. But he'd only gone a few yards when he slowed down to listen more carefully. The engine sounded wrong. It was making a heavy, clanking, thumping noise. It could hardly be a car. It had to be a truck, or a tractor, or some other heavy farm vehicle.

Before he knew what he was doing, Peter raced back to his cave, instinctively wanting to hide himself. The tractor came nearer, the roar of its engine echoing loudly round the bare rock. Peter drew back out of sight as it passed, and caught only a glimpse of yellow paintwork and the blue and red checked shirt of its driver.

He waited for the noise to die away, but it droned on as loudly as ever. The tractor seemed to have stopped. Carefully, making sure he was hidden by the elder bush growing by the entrance to the cave, Peter parted the branches and peered through them.

The farmer had jumped down to open the gate into the field behind the cave. He came back, and was about to climb up into the driving seat again, when he seemed to change his mind. He looked round, then fiddled with his fly button and disappeared round the corner. Peter heard a splashing noise as he urinated, and the man grunting as he zipped himself up.

Then suddenly he appeared again, very close. Peter almost let go of the bushes and darted back into the cave, sure that the man would hear the pounding of his heart, but he stopped himself in time. The movement would have been bound to attract attention.

Peter willed himself to keep still. He could see the man clearly now. He was stocky, and under his old cloth cap, his face was weatherbeaten and leathery, the skin deeply crinkled round the eyes. He was dressed like most of the country Frenchmen Peter had seen in the village cafés, in old blue dungarees over his checked shirt, the sleeves of which were rolled back above muscular forearms.

Peter was steeling himself to step out and say "*Bonjour, je m'appelle Pierre,*" when the man turned slightly, and Peter saw the scar that ran down the side of his right cheek, pulling his lip up into an unpleasant leer. At the same moment his mother's endlessly repeated warnings came back to him.

"Don't talk to strangers. There are all sorts of funny people about. Keep yourself to yourself. Never hang around in lonely places. There's safety in numbers."

The farmer climbed back onto the tractor, drove through the gate into the field, jumped off and shut it behind him, then clattered away up the hillside and over the crest out of sight. The noise died away.

{5}

When the tractor had gone, Peter sat down on his boulder and burst into tears. He felt so desolate, he wrapped his arms round himself and rocked backwards and forwards for comfort.

"I'm all alone," he kept repeating. "And I'm lost. And they couldn't be bothered to check if I was with them. And they'll never find me."

He cried for quite a long time. At last, he lifted his head and wiped his nose on the bottom of his T-shirt.

A flickering movement caught his eye. A lizard, which had been basking in the afternoon sun on the rocky wall at the entrance to the cave, had been alarmed by his sudden movement, and had whisked itself into a crevice.

It must live here, thought Peter. The cave must be its home.

"It's all right," he said out loud to the lizard. "I won't hurt you."

It was as if the lizard had understood. It darted out of its hiding place and returned to bask, its small diamond shaped head, angular legs, curved body and tapering tail as motionless as a carving.

I suppose that's the bit of rock he lives on, thought Peter. It's sort of like his sitting-room.

He moved cautiously. The lizard didn't run away this

time. It no longer seemed frightened of him.

He's quite friendly, thought Peter. A lot more my friend than Julian Fletcher, anyway.

The lizard shifted a little, turning its body more fully to the sun. As it did so, an idea hit Peter head-on.

Why can't I live here too? Really live here, like it says in my survival book?

He'd had his survival book for his birthday, last May, and had read it through again and again, from cover to cover. Then he'd lent it to Simon, at school, who kept on forgetting to give it back.

The most interesting sections of the book were on trapping wild animals and making a fire. Peter could almost recite the instructions on how to snare a rabbit, how to trap a bird, and how to set a night line for fish. He'd imagined himself doing it all, down to the cooking and eating. He'd tried to follow the diagrams for making different kinds of knots. He'd studied the pictures of which plants were edible and which were poisonous. He'd frequently tried to make fire by rubbing sticks together, without success.

"I could do it," he said. "I could catch my food, and make a proper bed, and set this cave up properly. And they'd be really really sorry when they found me, if they ever do."

He looked round the cave with new eyes, taking possession of it. There was a convenient, cupboard-like hole at eye level that he'd noticed when he'd first come into the cave. The shadows made it hard to see how deep the hole was. He ran his fingers over the whole surface.It was smaller than he'd thought.

I bet cavemen kept their arrows and bits of bone and best flints here, he thought. He poked into every corner, hoping to find something, but all he came up with was an ancient piece of silver paper. Bits had been nibbled off round the edges by some animal or insect, and the sheen had dulled to a lifeless grey.

He suddenly seemed to hear his mother's voice, talking across the fence to Maggie Cooper, the woman next door, as she probably would tomorrow.

"We found this wonderful little place for our picnic, in the middle of France somewhere, right off the beaten track."

Couldn't be further off the beaten track than this, he thought. If it was on it, there'd be broken glass, and crisp packets. And people would have peed in here. The cave's remoteness half pleased and half worried him.

As he turned away from the hole, something caught his eye. Something was moving near his feet. He bent down to look. An ant was carrying a vast leaf, six or seven times its own size, across the floor of the cave. The leaf stuck straight up in the air like a sail.

"Oh, no," said Peter. "Lizards, yes. But not insects."

He went outside and snapped some fronds off the elder bush, remembering just in time to take them from the back, where the broken ends couldn't be seen by a passer-by. The ant had disappeared, but he swept the floor all the same, and gathered up the loose sticks and stones, chucking them into a pile at the back of the cave under the green funnel.

The roof sloped down more steeply on one side than on the other, then it seemed to level off, making a crevice about half a metre high and two or three metres long. The shadows were so dark it was impossible to see how far back the space ran.

Peter had bent down to peer into the crevice when he'd first come into the cave, but he hadn't wanted, somehow, to creep inside it. The darkness in there was too dark, the stillness too still. Since he'd swept out the rest of the cave, and had touched every corner of it with his broom, it had become truly his. He knew it, and owned it. But the crevice was still outside his realm. It was a threat, alien and unexplored.

"I'll have to go in," he muttered. "I can't live in here, not knowing what's behind my back."

He got down on his hands and knees and put his head inside.

At least there's no draught, he thought, so there can't be a tunnel leading off somewhere.

His eyes were slowly adjusting to the darkness. He could pick out some pale pebbles on the floor, and the faint shape of the rock on the farther wall. He ran his hands over the rock roof. There was nothing odd there. It was smooth and rounded, rising to a low dome.

The ground was covered with loose stones. He reached back into the main cave for his broom of fronds, and started sweeping. It was easier to advance into the darkness if he swept the floor before him as he went.

In a little while he was right inside. He could sit up now. His skin contracted in a shudder when he saw how low the roof was at the entrance point, and how long it would take him to crawl out again if he needed to in a hurry. He forced himself not to think of it.

His eyes were seeing more all the time. It was surprising how much he could pick out, using the faint glimmer that reflected into the crevice from the main cave. It wasn't so frightening now. It was like being in a cupboard at the back of a room, empty, quiet and safe. Slowly he began to relax. Perhaps I could sleep in here, he thought doubtfully.

Then he saw two small dark holes at the edge of the floor where the roof came down to touch it.

"Snakes!" he whispered. It was as if an alarm bell had rung in his head. Frantically he began to scramble backwards out of the crevice.

{6}

A mile away from the cave, where the stream ran into a small lake, Monsieur Maurice Gérard, the retired schoolmaster and present mayor of the commune and village of St Didier-des-Bois, was sitting on a neat fold-away stool in the pleasant shade of a large oak tree, impaling a maggot on his fish-hook. He looked up over his spectacles when he heard a tractor approach, and waved when he saw who was driving it.

The tractor slowed down and stopped beside him. Maurice Gérard reeled out his line, stood up, and deftly cast it. It landed satisfactorily in the precise spot where, a few seconds earlier, a plump carp had jumped out of the water, its body raining a shower of iridescent drops.

Monsieur Roland Favier, the tractor driver, watched critically until the operation was completed.

"Is that a new rod, Maurice? Where'd you get it? Not at old Gaillard's place, I bet."

Maurice Gérard sat down on his stool again, removed a well-laundered handkerchief from the pocket of his fishing jacket, and mopped his perspiring forehead.

"Not much good my going to the trouble of getting a decent rod with this pond in the state it's in. It's infested with catfish. When are you going to do something about it, Roland? That's what I want to know."

Roland Favier switched off the engine of the tractor, which had been idling noisily.

"I can't do it on my own. It needs at least ten men. You know that. We'll have to drain the whole pond like we did five years ago. You remember – it was a cold day and old Lucien fell in. He was soaked to the skin. Nearly died of pneumonia."

The line juddered in Monsieur Gérard's hands. Both men waited expectantly, but it went slack again.

"Your damned catfish've probably stolen my bait," grumbled Monsieur Gérard, expertly reeling in. "This used to be a good pond in your father's day. Properly maintained. Fat carp as long as your arm."

Sensitive to this criticism, Roland Favier snorted.

"That's hardly my fault, is it? It was foreigners put those catfish in. It was those thieving louts from Moulins who camped down at the mill the year my barn caught fire. They did it for revenge because I told them to clear off my land. And if you'd provided a proper municipal camp site, instead of sitting round on your backside for ten years talking about it, they'd never have been trespassing on my land in the first place."

Maurice Gérard was not at all put out.

"Ah, but we did provide one, didn't we? And very popular it's proved too. They're back."

"What? Who's back?"

"Your thieving louts."

"*My . . .?*" Roland Favier was lost for words.

"They won't cause you any trouble. Seemed quite

amenable in fact. They're only here for a bit, they told me, having a little summer holiday. Then they'll be off back to Moulins again."

Monsieur Favier was not interested in the campers' future plans.

"No trouble?" he exploded. "No *trouble*? Gates left open, carp poached from the pond, trout stolen from the stream, leeks nicked from my vegetable garden, fires started –"

"You had no proof about who burnt down your barn," said Monsieur Gérard, carefully refolding his handkerchief and replacing it in his pocket. "Anyway, the way you threatened them you must have scared them silly. That scar of yours is enough to terrify anyone. It even gives me nightmares sometimes."

Roland Favier fingered his cheek.

"Honourable wounds," he said, quoting his citation. "Received in . . ."

". . . the course of duty, I know."

They fell silent for a moment. In their youth they'd been soldiers together. It was Maurice Gérard who had pulled Roland Favier clear of their bombed out lorry in the Algerian desert. They'd been arguing when the lorry had run over the mine. They argued during the rescue. They'd argued ever since. They were the closest friends.

"I can't stay here, wasting time," said Monsieur Favier, climbing back onto his tractor. "Some of us have got work to do."

"I'll drop by at the camp site on the way home," said

Monsieur Gérard. "I'll tell them what a terror you are when it comes to little matters like poaching, and fires being lit on your land. I'll put the fear of God into them.

"And I'll go round and do an extra check this evening. I've just been along the lane by the cave.It's quiet enough there, anyway. Not a soul about."

Monsieur Favier started his engine and the tractor's big yellow wheels began to churn up the dust. He looked back and waved at his friend.

Maurice Gérard was on his feet, excitedly reeling in his line. Six inches of wriggling silver shot out of the water. Even at a distance, Roland Favier could make out the thick whiskers that stuck out from the fish's flat jaw. He grunted with amusement at the expression of disgust on his friend's face.

"Poor old Maurice. Another flaming catfish."

{7}

Peter recovered from his panic as soon as he was out of the crevice. He stood in the cave looking down at the long dark slit he'd just crawled out of, feeling foolish.

Why had he suddenly thought of snakes? He hadn't seen or heard anything suspicious in there. Now that he was out once more in the cave, which he knew for sure was safe and empty, he could think it over rationally. Surely the holes he'd seen couldn't be deep enough for a whole long snake to wriggle into? The walls and floors of the crevice were made of hard rock, with only a fine dusting of sand in the hollows.

"I've got to find out," he said to himself. The doubt was worse than anything.

He went to the pile of debris he'd left at the back of the cave under the green funnel. He chose a long stick with some sap still in it and bent it to test its strength between his hands. It bowed but didn't snap. Then he went back to the entrance to the crevice, lay down on the floor of the cave, and peered in.

He could see the two holes on the far side quite clearly. He aimed the stick at the first hole, fighting down the horror that was making his flesh creep. The stick didn't quite reach. He wriggled forward, ready to back out at speed if necessary, and gingerly poked it into the hole. It met solid rock a couple of inches in. He'd been holding his breath without realizing it. Now he let it out in a rush. More confidently, he tried the other hole. It was a little deeper than the first, but still no more than a slight dent in the rock.

It's just the way the light falls that makes them look so scary, he thought. There's nothing there at all. Only shadows.

He backed out again, sweating with relief. The crevice was no longer a dark unknown, a threat out of which frightening things might crawl. It was his now, a secret place, a room within a room.

That's my shelter sorted out, he thought. Now for food. I've got to think about food. Good thing I had so much lunch. I probably won't feel hungry for hours.

Immediately, he did feel hungry. He wasn't ravenous, or desperate. He just had a nagging desire to eat, and the more he thought about it, the worse it became.

He remembered Sophie and Rachel picking blackberries down by the stream. He'd start by doing the same. Blackberries weren't filling exactly, but they'd be better than nothing. They were juicy as well, and would stop him feeling thirsty.

As he went outside he looked for the lizard on its sitting stone. There were two there now. The second was smaller. It was silver with a bright green stripe running down its back.

"Hello, Stripey," said Peter. The silver lizard scuttled off into a clump of overhanging grass. The other stayed.

"Hi, Robert," said Peter. "You're not scared of me, are you?"

The lizard did not move.

"Robert," said Peter again. It sounded right, he didn't know why. He was glad he'd given them names. It made them seem even more friendly.

The blackberries were growing thickly along the hedges that bordered the lane and ran down to the stream. Rachel and Sophie had eaten them out near the picnic spot, but further along they were plentiful and ripe, glowing lustrous and purple in the strong light of the late afternoon sun.

It was different in France. People didn't seem to think much of blackberries. They let them fall.

He picked and ate until he was bored. It was fiddly and irritating, having to reach up and risk being scratched for every morsel, but although he'd soon eaten several handfuls he didn't feel satisfied.

I've got to get some real food, he thought. Some meat, or potatoes, or something.

He licked his juice-stained fingers and went back to the cave. He sat down on his boulder and thought about his survival book. He could visualize his favourite pages, the section on trapping and stalking wild animals. He'd read them again and again, had imagined himself creeping through a wood after a deer, or sitting up over a rabbit snare, but now that the moment had come to hunt a living, breathing animal, with fur and blood and teeth and claws, he wasn't sure. Tomorrow he could try something like that. It would take too long today. He had to find food quickly, before night fell.

He tried to remember the section on edible plants. He'd only skimmed over it a few times. It had been too like a school nature book. But now he racked his memory. Chickweed was edible, he knew that. He'd fed it to his gerbils often enough. So were dandelions, and stinging nettles. He could see some of the other drawings of plants in his mind's eye. The only problem was he couldn't remember which ones had a skull printed alongside them, and the large word POISONOUS in heavy black print. He'd have to stick to the ones he was sure of. Come to think of it, he'd seen nettles down by the stream. They'd have to be cooked, of course, to get rid of the stings.

Cooking meant making a fire. He could have a go at that. The survival book suggested several methods. He'd tried them all out at home – rubbing sticks together, using a flint and a steel bolt, refracting the sun's rays through a magnifying glass. He'd never managed to get a proper fire going, but he would just have to try, try, and try again until he managed it.

He looked down the lane. There was plenty of fuel. The countryside had been baked to a tinder dryness by the hot summer sun. Dried up leaves, wisps of hay and frail, brittle twigs lay everywhere along the grassy verges. He got up, and within a few minutes had collected a good armful. He'd lay his fire not where he'd first thought, at the mouth of the cave, but at the back, under the green funnel. It would be hidden there. The smoke would filter out through the undergrowth above, and with luck would be unseen to anyone passing along the lane.

He dumped the fuel on the ground. It was too soon to think of lighting it. He had to find some food to cook on it first, and, just as important, he had to find something to cook it in. He needed a pot or a kettle of some kind.

His book had shown him how he could cook quite well in an old tin can, making a handle, and a tripod to hang it from. He'd look for one later on, by the stream. In England, streams seemed to attract litter like bright lights attracted moths. He couldn't remember seeing any here, but it would be worth a try.

The first thing was to collect some stuff to cook. He would leave the nettles till last, as he knew where to find them anyway, and look for chickweed and dandelions.

His mouth puckered at the thought of dandelions. He'd nibbled some once before, after he'd read about people eating them in a story. They tasted revolting. Still, he had no choice.

I'd better get a move on, he thought. It would probably take hours to gather enough for even a small meal. He'd look out for a tin can too. Something hot and cooked, even if it was just a funny tasting soup, would be nicer to eat than a load of raw leaves.

{8}

"Stop the car, Mum. I'm bursting."

"Oh Rachel, really! Can't you wait?"

"No, honestly, I'm dying!"

"But we'll lose sight of Dad and Billie. I want to change drivers when we stop for petrol. I don't fancy driving round the *périphérique* on my own. In rush-hour."

"My mum's scared of French motorways too," said Sophie.

"Scared?" said Mrs Castle. "I'm not scared. I'm just not used to them, that's all."

"Oo!" shrieked Rachel. "Quick! I can't wait any longer!"

Mrs Castle swung the car over onto the hard shoulder and braked sharply. Rachel scrabbled at the handle, opened the door and raced into a thin screen of bushes, tugging at her shorts as she went.

Mrs Castle kept the engine running, ready to start off again the moment Rachel was back. She didn't hear the police car glide to a stop behind her. She didn't hear anything until a polite, official voice at her elbow said, *"Bonjour, Madame."*

She jumped and turned to look into the face of a tall policeman.

"Oh," she said helplessly. "Er, *bonjour*."

He touched the peak of his cap. He was not smiling, but he didn't look unfriendly.

"Vous êtes en panne?"

"Je suis anglais," said Mrs Castle. "English. No understand."

The policeman's shorter co-driver came up to join him.

"What's up?"

"Tourists. Don't speak French. How's your English?"

The other took a step backwards.

"Oh no. I'm not going to make a fool of myself. Come on, Devaux, you're the intellectual."

Rachel scampered back to the car and jumped in on the far side. The two policemen didn't notice her. They'd walked round to look at the front of the car.

"There you see?" said Mrs Castle. "Now you've got us into a right mess. It's probably illegal to stop on the motorway. We'll probably be arrested. Just look at them! Now they're checking on the registration plate. They could hold us here for hours, checking papers, searching us even. And the ferry goes at eight!" Her voice was becoming shrill.

Sergeant Devaux bent down to see if either front tyre was punctured.

"See anything?" his colleague said.

"No. Perhaps it's the brakes. Or the clutch. The engine's running all right."

"Could be either. We'd better check it out. We can't let her drive off down the autoroute if anything's wrong.

Not with a couple of kids on board."

"I'll ask her to get out then."

He went round to the driver's door, opened it, and indicated with a flourish of his hand that he wanted Mrs Castle to get out.

"Oh, my God," she groaned. She'd gone pale. "She looks terrified," said the shorter policeman. "She probably thinks we're arresting her."

Devaux smiled reassuringly at Mrs Castle.

"Madame, out please. Test – uh – *voiture*."

Comprehension dawned on Mrs Castle's face.

"Voiture? Oh, there's nothing wrong with the car. Motor – OK. Voiture – OK."

Devaux raised his shoulders and spread out his hands in a gesture of enquiry.

"Rachel," said Mrs Castle over her shoulder, "if you ever do this to me again I'll disown you."

She looked up at the policeman again and pointed into the back of the car.

"*Ma fille*. Er . . . She had to go to the toilet."

The sergeant clearly did not understand.

"WC. Toilet. In the bushes." She pointed to the undergrowth nearby. "Psss," she added desperately.

"Ah!"

Devaux laughed and slapped his hand against the roof of the car. Then he assumed his official expression, and bent once more to the window.

"Madame," he said seriously. "*Vous êtes en France*. No permit *toilette* on the autoroute."

"Sorry," said Mrs Castle. "*Pardon.*" She sensed she was about to be let off, and smiled ingratiatingly. Devaux straightened up.

"*Bon, allez-y*. You go," he said, and returned with his colleague to their waiting car.

Mrs Castle let in the clutch and nosed gingerly out into the slow stream. Her hands were shaking.

Three miles further on, Mr Castle had just presented his credit card at the cash desk of the petrol station. He was looking over his shoulder, keeping an eye on the passing traffic. He turned to sign the docket, took the receipt and jogged back to Billie who was sitting in the car.

"Any sign of them? Did you see them pass?"

"No. There've only been two with GB numberplates, haven't there, Julian? And they were both Ford fiestas."

Mr Castle frowned.

"That's funny. They were right behind us until a mile or so back. I wish I'd brought my mobile. I just didn't want the office contacting me all the time." He glanced at Billie, but she was examing the chipped varnish on her nails. "I wonder if anything's happened? Perhaps we'd better turn round."

Billie wound her window up

"I'm sure they're fine. They probably stopped for a snack in a lay-by or something. You know what the girls are like."

"Yes, but Rosemary'll want to follow me when we get

nearer Paris. She won't want to do the *périphérique* on her own."

Billie pulled a scarf out of her handbag and tied it over her hair.

"You know what, Tom? You worry too much. Rosemary'll manage fine. She's a big girl. And anyway, don't you remember? You said "See you at Calais". She won't be looking out for you till we get there."

"No, perhaps not." Mr Castle started the engine and drove onto the slip road. "All the same . . ."

They lapsed into an uncomfortable silence.

{9}

Peter ran purposefully across the field and down to the stream, making up a plan as he went. He'd walk along by the water's edge, more or less parallel with the lane, in the opposite direction from the way he'd gone before, when he'd been chasing the car. For one thing, the vegetation was bound to be thicker near the water, and he'd be more likely to find edible plants. For another, he might find a decent place to fish. The parts of the stream he'd seen so far had seemed too shallow and fast-running to be much good for fishing. At the same time, he'd keep a look out for any useful junk he could use as containers or utensils for cooking.

Almost at once he had an amazing piece of luck. A short way downstream, a low outcrop of rock, of the same whitish, gnarled kind from which his cave was formed, jutted out of the opposite hillside, making the stream bend sharply.

Peter quickly scanned the plants growing at the base of the rock. They looked prickly and inedible. Nothing much there, he thought. Not worth crossing the stream for.

Then he heard something. It was the sound of water – not the rippling, slurping noise of the stream tumbling over its pebbly bed, but a dripping, dribbling sound, as if a tap had been left half-on. It was coming from the outcrop, near its base.

The stream was wide and shallow at this point, where it opened out round the bend. It was quite easy for Peter to pick his way across a natural path of stepping stones without getting his feet wet.

The ground on the other side was soft and marshy, but even here there were enough flat stones to stand on without having to step into the mud. Peter carefully parted the thorny briar stems, peered at the rock behind them, and grunted with satisfaction.

Water, crystal clear and as clean as country rain, was welling out of the rock in huge, regular tears. Peter cupped his hands, let the water fill them, and drank it. It was cold and delicious. He felt elated, as if he had won a race, or been given one hundred per cent in a test.He knew from his book that a clean water supply was the most vital thing of all if you had to survive in the wild. A person could live for weeks without food if they had plenty of water to drink. There had been the stream of course, but he hadn't fancied drinking from that. He'd seen sheep droppings right beside it, and anyway, all kinds of rotten or polluting things might have been dumped in it higher up.

He drank and drank, until he got bored with waiting for his cupped hands to fill. The water seemed to clear his head and sharpen his eyes. He crossed back over the stream. Immediately, he noticed a clump of long, serrated dandelion leaves, the first he'd recognised. He'd been looking out for the yellow flowers, or the fluffy clocks.

Of course, he thought. They've probably stopped flowering now, it'll be autumn soon.

The leaves were thick and tough-looking, a hard dark green. He picked one, and nibbled a bit off the end. It tasted horrible. Bravely, he forced himself to cram the rest into his mouth, chew, and swallow.

The triumph he'd felt when he found the spring had burnt itself out. I can't live on stuff like this, he thought.

He saw suddenly, in his mind's eye, a plateful of real food, a giant hamburger and a mound of mashed potato, a fruit dish beside it, piled high with bananas and apples, brimming over with grapes. Determinedly, he pushed the vision away.

I'll show them, he thought. I'll manage here. They'll be sorry. I'll show them.

Anger made him feel better. It lifted him again. He took another look at the dandelion clump.

No, he thought. Not raw, anyway. I could try them in a soup, I suppose, when I've found a can and made a fire.

Suddenly, he felt a sense of urgency. The sun was quite low now. He looked at his watch. Six o'clock. He had two-and-a-half hours at best until darkness fell. He had to find a can to cook his soup in, and plants to make it with. He had to find fish, and think out a way of catching them. He had to make a fire.

The banks of the stream, once past the rocky outcrop, were more thickly wooded than they were near the cave.

Willows bent over the water, their long branches trailing in the current. Past the trees, the field narrowed to a point, and the stream met the lane and passed under it, beneath a low bridge. Peter peered along the stream as far as he could. Filtered sunlight played on the surface, making shimmering herring-bone patterns in the water, but there was no welcome glint of metal or cellophane, no sign of rubbish at all.

I'll look along the lane, he thought. I might be luckier there.

He wriggled through a gap in the hedge, and broke into a trot, his eyes scanning the ditch on either side as he went. About a hundred metres further on there was another gap, filled by a rickety gate. The screws holding its hinges to the rotten post had long since rusted into uselessness, and the farmer had done a makeshift mending job with wire.

Peter looked at it closely. He needed wire. He needed it to make a pot handle. He'd need it to make snares, when he set about hunting rabbits in the morning. He'd need it to hold his woven door in place, if he ever got around to finishing it.

There seemed to be several generations of wire on the gatepost. It looked as if, whenever one lot had worked loose, the farmer had simply wound a new piece round beside it, without bothering to remove the old one. There were two good, sensible lengths which could easily be taken without making the gate fall over.

Quickly, Peter started to unravel them. One was

rusted and almost fell to bits as he moved it. The other was perfect. It was thick enough to be strong and hold its spring, but thin enough to bend easily. Peter held it out to its full length. There was about a metre of it, a good, manageable amount. He looped it up to make it easier to carry. Then he pushed at the gate to make sure it was still securely attached to its post. It was.

Encouraged, he set off again, sure that his luck was now in, and that the perfect can lay around the next corner.

There was indeed a surprise round the next corner, but it wasn't an empty can. It was the sound of music, coming from a radio or TV, from behind a spinney of scrubby oak trees a little way further along.

{10}

The municipal camp site, pride of Monsieur Gérard's mayorial heart, and object of Monsieur Favier's suspicion, occupied an attractive area of flat, grassy land in a bend of the stream, half-a-mile away from the cave. The ground had been levelled off. Fresh water had been laid on and some basic sanitation installed.

Only one trailer was in occupation at present, a small rented one. It was parked in the shade of the only tree, an old walnut. A makeshift awning, supported on rickety metal props, ran from its door, and a folding table and three camping chairs were set up underneath it.

Madame Bourlaud was doing her washing. She held a boy's T-shirt up and looked at the stains which dotted its once white front. She rubbed at them half-heartedly a few times, then gave up and wrung it out.

Call this a holiday, she thought wearily. A holiday for my washing-machine at home, more like.

She threw the soapy water out in a shining arc across the grass, filled the bowl with clear water from the standpipe and returned to the table with it. Every time she moved she had to step over her husband's outstretched legs. Monsieur Bourlaud was lying back in his cushioned reclining chair with his straw hat pulled down over his eyes.

"And Stéphane's run off on his own again," Madame Bourlaud said, knowing he would not answer. "God only knows what he's getting up to."

She hadn't wanted to come here, but as her opinion was never asked for, and she didn't dare offer it of her own accord, Monsieur Bourlaud had followed his own inclinations as usual. The camp site down by the seaside, where they'd gone for the last two years, had been much more to her liking. There had been shops to look round, a cinema and a launderette. She'd met some friendly people, women to chat to while the men went off to the cafés. If only Jean-Pierre hadn't been such a fool, raising hell with the other boys, getting them expelled from two camp sites in the space of a week, they could have been back there now.

She'd finished pegging up her last towel and looked around. There wasn't a breath of wind in this close, tree-lined valley. It was airless and exhaustingly hot. If there had only been some other campers here it would have been better. As it was, she was stuck with a husband who went off poaching all day, or sat slumped in his chair, and a child who only appeared at mealtimes.

"Stéphane!" she called, knowing it was pointless. "Where the hell are you?"

She went back to the trailer and stepped gingerly over Monsieur Bourlaud's legs again. He was always bad-tempered if he was woken prematurely.

She was only just past him when he stirred and sat up of his own accord.

"Who's this then?" he said, rubbing the sleep out of his eyes. She turned to see a small Citroën, sparkingly clean, pulling up at the entrance to the camp site.

"Other people coming, I expect," said Madame Bourlaud hopefully.

"Don't be daft." Monsieur Bourlaud stood up and scratched his armpit. "It's that old fool of a mayor." He put on a prissy voice. "Oh hello, Monsieur. I hope you are deeply grateful for this wonderful camp site I have so generously provided for you."

Maurice Gérard approached them over the grass, carefully skirting the wet patch where Madame Bourlaud's washing water hadn't yet soaked into the hard ground.

"*Bonjour, Monsieur,*" he said, his soft cheeks creased in a beaming smile. "Back again, I see?"

"As you see."

"Camp site to your liking?"

"Oh yes. Very good. Very clean."

"I am sure you'll make every effort to leave it that way. Staying long?"

"A week or so."

"I hope you'll find enough to amuse you. And to keep the children busy."

"Oh, you know, we are here to relax, to rest . . ."

"Young minds, Monsieur, are lively. They need to be kept occupied. To be kept out of mischief. I'm sure you will be interested to hear that Monsieur Favier has only just managed to get his barn rebuilt."

"I don't know what you're talking about." Monsieur

Bourlaud thrust his head forward pugnaciously.

"Jean-Pierre isn't here this year," interrupted Madame Bourlaud hastily, ruining the effect. "He's . . ." On the spur of the moment she couldn't think how to explain his absence. "He's in Moulins," she finished lamely.

"In custody already?" said Monsieur Gérard with undiminished cheerfulness. "Dear me." He saw he'd hit the nail on the head.

"I'm sure we all want to avoid any unnecessary unpleasantness," he went on, as if he was addressing a classroom full of rowdy adolescents, "so I've come to give you a little advice."

Monsieur Bourlaud's face expressed a subtle blend of injured innocence and derision.

"Yes, Monsieur. Advice. We're running a campaign in this commune, with the enthusiastic co-operation of our good friends at the gendarmerie, to stamp out poaching, petty theft, and other misdemeanours. Anyone who is caught will be charged at once and subject to the severest penalties."

"Poaching? Petty theft?" Monsieur Bourlaud managed to give the impression that he'd never heard the words before.

"If you wish to fish, you will need a permit. Try the people up at the château." He waved his arm in the vague direction of a wooded hill a short distance away. "They're Parisians – new in these parts. Only here for the weekend. You might be lucky. Don't waste your time asking Monsieur Favier for permission to fish in his lake.

I know for a fact that he is not inclined to oblige you."

He puffed out his cheeks, lowered himself into the driving seat of his car, and waved a genial farewell.

"Pompous prat," snorted Monsieur Bourlaud. He turned on his wife. "Fine help you were!"

"I'm sorry, Roger. I . . ."

"You can shut your trap and get the barbecue out. You bought those steaks, like I told you to this morning? I could fancy a nice bit of meat tonight."

"Supper already?" said Madame Bourlaud. "But Stéphane's not back yet. He . . ."

"If he's not here, he doesn't get any. It's quite simple. The way you spoil him, he'll end up like that other precious son of yours – in the nick."

He went into the caravan, turned up the volume on the TV, then settled himself back in his chair and resumed his nap.

{11}

Peter stopped dead in his tracks when he heard the music. It sounded so cheerful and normal, so comfortingly home-like, that he wanted to run straight towards it and shout, "Hello! I'm lost! Can you help me?" But he stayed where he was, standing still in the lane.

He felt confused. "I can't speak French," he told himself. "What's the good of trying to explain?"

It was only an excuse, and he knew it. He could ask for help. He could make himself understood if he really wanted to, but he had a picture in his mind of his parents, finding him at last in the cave where they had callously abandoned him, after a long, agonising search. It would be much better if they found him there alone. His anger fed on the idea. Then, too, there was the pull of the cave itself. His cave. He wanted to live in it, make something of it, survive in it.

The music stopped. A voice came on. It sounded fast and jokey, as if it was presenting a games show or a comedy programme. Peter's resolve weakened. I'll get a bit closer. Have a good look, he thought. He had in his mind's eye a TV set sitting by an open window in an old farmhouse, like the one they'd been staying at in the Dordogne, with a few flowers in a half-barrel outside, and some chickens pecking about in the dusty courtyard.

He clambered over a fence of slack barbed wire and entered the spinney. Instinctively he went silently, as if he was a wild animal, treading only where the bare earth had no covering of twigs that could snap or leaves that could rustle. The TV voice was getting louder all the time.

He reached the far side of the wood and peered through the screen of bushes that edged it. A camp site! He almost laughed out loud. There were bound to be English people here. In every camp site in the Dordogne half the cars seemed to have GB number plates. Mum had got quite irritated sometimes. "Might as well be in Scarborough," she'd kept on saying.

If there are English people here, thought Peter, I suppose it would be silly not to speak to them.

He stepped sideways to get a better view. He'd thought at first there were several cars and caravans, but now he could see that there was only one. He moved again, and then he saw a man. He was sleeping in a reclining camping chair, a hat pulled down over his eyes. A woman came out from the shadow of the awning that stretched out from the door of the trailer. She stepped over the man's legs with care.

Peter could see at once that she wasn't English. There was something about her dress and her shoes – even in the way she carried the clothes basket on her hip – that told him she was French, and a glance at the number plate on the old white car confirmed it.

His heart sank as he watched her walk over to the washing line. She had a defeated look about her. Her fair hair had been permed some time ago, and now straggled, depressingly lank, over her shoulders. She was overweight, not in a comfortable, generous way, but unhealthily, as if her flesh was sagging with the heaviness of life's difficulties. Even from a distance he could see the bulbous network of varicose veins on her calves. He couldn't imagine her being much help if he tried to approach her.

The man grunted and stirred. Although he was asleep, Peter could sense the violence in him. He took another step back. Something clattered behind him. The noise sounded deafening to him, but the man didn't stir again, and the woman went on pegging out her washing, showing no sign of disturbance.

Peter looked down. His foot had hit a can, a beautiful, big, new, unrusted tin can. It nestled in a mess of broken glass and dirty polythene bags. He squatted down and carefully released it, easing it as quietly as he could away from the tinkling glass. Flies buzzed round the dried juice inside it. Underneath it was another, smaller can. He pulled that out too. Then he retrieved an empty plastic bottle lying a little further on. It would be useful for carrying water.

He stood up and crept back through the wood, forcing himself not to hurry in case he made a noise. Once out in the lane he began to run, his booty held carefully in his arms, looking over his shoulder as he went, certain he was being pursued.

Halfway back to the cave, the feeling of danger left

him and he slowed down to a walk. He felt gloriously triumphant. He'd solved the problem of the cooking pot. He was a step nearer to supper.

The light was becoming deeper now as the sun sank lower, and the colours of the sky, the grass and even the stones in the lane were glowing as if they were lit from in-side. It was easier to see the shapes of leaves and pick out different kinds of plants from the mass of stuff in the ditch.

He recognised a low tuft of chickweed, and pounced on it. There was enough to make a big bundle. A little further on was a clump of nettles. Most of them were old, but some new shoots were growing at one side, where someone had recently cut down the old ones. He picked up a stick and hacked at the stems, managing to slice off a good number of shoots. Then without touching them he manoeuvred them into the can with the tip of the stick. When the can was full, he ran back to the cave. He was ready to make his soup and light his fire.

There was no sign of Robert or Stripey on their stone near the cave's entrance. Peter was disappointed. He'd looked forward to the sight of their friendly little shapes. Then out of the corner of his eye he caught sight of a flickering movement overhead, and looked up. The two lizards were chasing each other across the roof of the entrance, stopping every now and then as if they were on a video, and someone had pressed the 'pause' button.

"There you are," said Peter with relief. "I'm going to get my supper ready now."

He picked up his can. It would need washing out before he could use it. He'd take it down to the spring, clean it and bring back some water for his soup before he tried to light the fire.

The pile of greens was beginning to wilt. It looked dull and unappetizing. If only I had my rod and line, thought Peter. I could get a fish.

He'd caught some quite big fish in the Dordogne, big enough for Mum to actually cook, though she'd grumbled that there was more fin and bone than flesh on any of them. His fishing gear was in the car, like everything else.

I couldn't make a rod, he thought. Not without a line, and hooks and a reel.

Then he remembered Rachel calling out to him when she and Sophie had run off towards the stream to play. Surely she'd said something about a dam?

That gave him an idea. He could make a fish trap, like they used to in the Stone Age. He knew roughly what to do. The first thing was to make the dam. Then you had to direct the water through a channel and into a system of stakes. The fish would have to go through the channel and the stakes would get narrower and narrower, ending in a kind of cage. The fish would be unable to turn round and swim out again.

I don't suppose the dam'll be much good if those two made it, he thought, even if they ever did.

He didn't want to think about Rachel, or remember her buttercup shorts prancing through the thistles. She was happily sitting in the car, behind Mum, playing her endless stupid clapping games. She was as guilty as the rest of them. When he saw her again he'd . . .

He dragged his mind back to the question of fish traps. He'd go down to the stream and have a look. It might just be worth a try.

{12}

"Stop talking, you two. I've got to concentrate. We've got to get off at the proper exit or we'll never find our way off this motorway. Look out for signs to Porte de la Chapelle."

"Porte what? How do you spell it?"

Mrs Castle told her.

Rachel looked out of the window. The traffic raced past at terrifying speed through the cuttings and tunnels of the Paris ring-road. There was nothing much to see. She breathed on the window and drew a picture in the condensation with her finger.

"Look, Soph."

Sophie looked and started giggling. She breathed on her own window and drew too. Her effort was even ruder than Rachel's. Both of them guffawed.

Mrs Castle's shoulders were hunched over the wheel but she turned and shouted in exasperation, "Didn't you hear what I said? Shut up!"

A car swerved right in front of her. She slammed her foot onto the brake pedal, and the car jerked forwards, catapulting the girls against their seat belts. A cacophany of horns blared behind her. She slowed down and cars shot past, their owners' hands raised in a variety of gestures expressing contempt and derision.

Rachel and Sophie were frightened into silence for the next five minutes.

"Over there, Mum, look! Porte whatever it is."

Mrs Castle removed her eyes from the road for the briefest possible moment to look at the sign.

"Wrong porte, but it's the next one. Any minute now."

She'd got herself into the left hand lane and needed to be in the right one to get down the slip road. She put on her indicator lights and tried to pull over but a huge lorry, travelling at the same speed, was in the way. She didn't have time to overtake and pull in front of it, and everytime she slowed down to try to get behind it, the impatient traffic behind her hooted at her to keep going. When at last she'd inched past the juggernaut, she let out a cry of anguish. "That's it! We've missed it! What on earth are we going to do now?"

"Missed what, Mum?"

"The turn off. The autoroute to Calais. And we're running late as it is. My God, when I get hold of your father . . ."

Mr Castle, stuck in a rush hour traffic jam a few miles north of Paris, was drumming his fingers on the rim of the steering wheel.

"We'll only just make it at this rate. Rosemary must be doing her nut."

Billie yawned. "There's always another ferry."

"Not till tomorrow morning, probably. And I don't fancy spending the night in a car park in Calais."

"Neither do I. I can think of much nicer places to spend it in."

Mr Castle frowned

"We shouldn't have let her get out of sight. We should have stayed together."

"I don't know what you're worrying about. We'll meet up at Calais."

"If we miss the ferry we won't know if Rosemary's ahead and has caught it, or if she's missed it too."

The car in front crawled forward. Mr Castle pressed the clutch down and put the car in gear. His foot slipped and the clutch came up in a rush. The car leaped ahead and almost hit the bumper of the car in front.

"Careful, Tom! What are you doing? You nearly hit them!" squealed Billie.

Mr Castle opened his car door, got out, walked round to the other side and opened the door of the passenger seat. The car in front moved forward again. The driver behind wound down his window and started shouting furiously. Mr Castle ignored him.

"Come on, Billie. Your turn to drive," he said coldly. "I've had enough. I'm tired."

She shrugged, undid her seat belt and got out. Without a word she sat down in the driver's seat and the car moved forward again.

"Mum," said Julian, "the batteries in my Walkman have run out. When are we going to get there?"

"How on earth should I know?" she snapped. "About the middle of next week I should think."

{13}

The dam was surprisingly good. The current had worked its way over the central section, washing away the weak wall of stones the girls had put up in its way, but the sides held well.

Peter could see at once how to make his trap. He would release the water at one side, where the bed was relatively free of rocks and stones. It would be much easier to ram sticks into the soft mud than into the stonier part in the middle.

He pulled off his trainers and socks and started at once, taking the stones off the side of the dam and putting them back in the middle. The water still gurgled through them, and minnows and such like could easily slip through, but a larger fish would have real problems. It would feel its way along the unexpected wall of stones, looking for an escape route, and the rush of water would carry it through the only open channel right into Peter's trap.

He'd just finished reorganizing the dam to his satisfaction when he saw his first proper fish. It was nosing along the stones just as he'd imagined it would, guiding itself with delicate flicks of its tail. The sun, glancing through the trees, caught its whippy movements for a moment as if in a spotlight, then the fish moved on into the shade and turned from silver back to dark grey.

I could just pick it up, thought Peter. He paddled frantically after it, plunged his hands into the water, felt its slippery skin and fluttering fins ripple through his hands, scrabbled frantically to hold on to it, almost losing his balance, and lost it. It slid on through the channel and away.

Why don't they teach us useful things at school, like tickling fish, he thought, instead of stupid geometry?

The fact that he'd been so close to catching a really good-sized fish encouraged him. He splashed out onto the bank and at once started looking for sticks. He would arrange them in a kind of funnel shape with a T-junction at the end, curling the horizontals of the T back and down, blocking the ends off to make two dead-end traps. He was absolutely sure it would work.

His first try was all wrong. The sticks were too short and weak. He hadn't allowed enough length to anchor them firmly in the mud, and he hadn't reckoned on the strength of the current. It simply knocked anything flimsy out of its path. He went back to the bank to look again. Nothing suitable was lying about. He would have to snap and cut branches from the trees.

There was no point in trying the willow. He knew from experience that it was stringy and flexible, too hard to cut and too bendy to stand against the current. An elder bush and a hazel tree were more promising. The thin branches were fairly easy to snap, and straight and stiff enough to make a reasonably sturdy wall.

It took much longer than he'd imagined. By the time the sticks were set up properly, far enough apart to allow the water to flow through, but close enough to catch a good-sized fish, his watch said 7.15. The sun was quite low now and the temperature was dropping. It was cool by the water and gnats were hovering in a hostile cloud above his head.

He wanted to stay and watch his trap, but he had an unpleasant sense that time was running out. He was also becoming extremely hungry.

I must make my fire, he thought. The lengthening shadows gave him an extra feeling of urgency. He needed his fire not only to cook his meal, but also as a weapon with which to fight the darkness.

He trotted on to the spring, his can in one hand, his bottle in the other, stopping only to pick and eat several more handfuls of blackberries.

Back at the cave, his precious supply of water carefully set down on a flat stone where it could not topple over, he examined his stock of firewood.

He'd tried to make fire before, in the garden at home. He'd rubbed sticks together, used a flint on steel, and made paper smoulder by holding a magnifying glass to the sun. He'd usually managed to produce charring, and even smoke, once or twice, but never an actual flame that took off and burned of its own accord. He thought he could do it. He *knew* he could do it if he tried hard enough, but he was very afraid that he would fail.

The most promising method had been the magnifying glass and paper one, but he couldn't use it this time. He had no magnifying glass, no paper, and the sun was too low. In fact, its great golden ball had gone down behind the trees already. Method number two was also impossible. He had no flint or steel. That left only the sticks, which he knew to be the hardest.

He chose a good, straight, hard stick and with his knife sharpened one end to a firm point.Then he ferreted around until he found a fairly large log, from which the bark had fallen off, exposing a good area of smooth core wood. He made a small dent in the top of it, squatted down, fitted the point into the dent and holding the stick between his hands, began to twist it backwards and forwards as fast as he could.

A few minutes later his shoulders were aching and the skin on his hands was sore. He stopped and looked at the point of the stick. There was no charring yet, but it felt warm. Then he realized that, even if he managed to make a spark, he hadn't provided any fuel for it to catch onto.

"Fool," he muttered.

He rummaged in his fuel pile, found what he was looking for, and made a little nest of dried grass and leaf fragments round the dent in the log. He started rubbing the stick between his hands again.

Suddenly he felt something on the back of his neck.

He put up a hand to brush it away. There was a furious buzzing noise and a hornet circled round his head. He flailed his arms at it and it veered away, then sailed out of the cave, its huge body quivering to a vicious hum.

Peter sat back on his heels. The hornet had scared him. There was a boy at school who was allergic to bees and hornets. He'd been stung on the hand once, in the middle of a cricket lesson. His hand had swollen up until it looked like a pink balloon with five sausages sticking out of it. The boy had gone blue round the lips and Mr Dexter had had to take him to hospital in his car for an emergency injection.

If I'm allergic, thought Peter, and a hornet gets me, I could die here, all on my own, and when they come they'll find my dead body.

He thought he heard the buzzing again. He stood up, scattering his fire-making equipment all over the floor of the cave.

"I'll do you!" he yelled. "You come back in here and I'll do you. I'll rip your wings off, do you hear – Fuzz Face?"

It was the silliest name he could think of. He flung it at the hornet, still hovering in the mouth of the cave, with utter contempt.

"Fuzz Face! Think you can sting? Think you can get away? I'll get you! Fuzz Face!"

The hornet flew away, and this time Peter could see that it had really gone. Its body was so big he could follow its flight path across the field, high above the trees that fringed the stream, black against the golden sky.

"Yeah, we did it, we scared him off," said Peter to Robert's tail, which could just be seen sticking out from under a large leaf, where the lizards had taken refuge when the action started.

Peter's triumph was short-lived. His fire-making stick had snapped in two where he'd trodden on it. The dent in the log showed no sign of burning. It was hardly warm.

Peter picked the stick up. It was too short now to be of any use and besides he didn't want to bring up blisters on his hands which felt bruised enough already.

That's it then, he thought. Without fire there would be no soup. Without soup he couldn't face the night here. He felt as if the cave had let him down, as if Robert and Stripey had abandoned him.

It'll have to be the camp site, I suppose. I'll have to give myself up.

He collected his anorak and knife, and looked round one last time. The lizards stayed obstinately out of sight.

"Be like that then," he said "I'm off."

His heart thudded uncomfortably as he walked towards the camp. He was trying to imagine the sleeping man's face turning out to be unexpectedly kind and friendly. He was trying to forget his mother's warnings. He was concentrating on the woman and the washing on the line. Surely child molesters and kidnappers didn't hang their washing out to dry?

I'd have been all right if I'd got the fire going, he thought. I wonder if there'll be any fish in the trap?

He nearly turned back to look, then he thought of trying to eat a raw fish, and carried on.

He decided to approach the camp through the wood again. That way he'd see without being seen. He could still back away if he wanted to.

He was halfway through the trees when a wonderful smell entered his nostrils. Someone was cooking meat on a barbecue. He could see it in his mind's eye – a thick, tender piece of steak, browned in places with little bubbles of juice spurting out of it. His mouth was producing so much water he had to swallow twice.

He was at the edge of the wood now, in his old place near the rubbish dump. He peered through the scrubby bushes. The woman was standing over the pan of glowing charcoal. She lifted some pieces of meat from the grill and took them over to the table set under the awning.

The moment her back was turned, a boy a few inches shorter than Peter, materialized as if out of the air, ran to the brazier, snatched up something from the ground beside it and dashed into the wood. Peter ducked behind a tree. The boy dived into the bushes, not more than a couple of metres from where Peter stood, lifted a plug of dry grass from the roots of a tree to reveal a hole in the ground, and dropped something into it.

A woman's thin, anxious voice called out, *"Stéphane! Viens manger! Où es tu?"*

The boy hurriedly replaced the grass and darted off. Peter watched him change gear as soon as he was out of the trees, slowing to a casual saunter, then slip into a chair by the table while the man's voice grumbled on and on over his head.

Peter went over to the tree and lifted the clump of grass. In the hole was a torch, an old newspaper, and a box of matches.

{14}

Peter didn't stop to think. The matches were in his jeans pocket and the paper in his hand before he knew what he was doing. He nearly took the torch. His hand reached out for it and then drew back. If he took the torch it would be a real give-away. The boy might easily think that a squirrel or a fox had run off with the matches, especially if he found the grass all messed up, but he would know that only a human could have taken the torch. He would hunt for it.

What does he want all this stuff for? thought Peter.

Moving silently, his ears alert to pick up any sound of an approach from the family, he picked the newspaper out of the hole. He took a large sheet, folded it as quietly as he could and tucked it into his belt. It would be useful in lighting the fire. The rest of the paper he tore to pieces, crumpled artistically and scattered about as a wild animal would have done. The torch he rolled deeper into the hole where a questing snout could have pushed it, then he messed up the plug of grass and left it nearby. He even tore off a little of the matchbox and dropped it by the hole, as if an animal had worried at it. The boy would never suspect a human thief.

Then, not wishing to stay close to danger any longer than he could help, Peter tiptoed back through the wood and jogged along the lane towards the cave.

He was thinking about the boy, trying to remember exactly what he'd looked like. He'd been quite small and thin, and his hair had been a thick dark thatch. He'd run with a kind of graceful precision, like a wild animal.

Bet he wants to run away, thought Peter. Bet that's why he's hiding stuff. He shared a moment of fellow feeling with the other boy, and his mood, which had been swinging from despair to jubilation and back again throughout the afternoon, rocketed up again. He felt confident enough to tackle anything.

He was puffed out by the time he got back to the cave and was sweating all over. Although the sun was setting properly now, the air was still very hot. The day had been a scorcher and the heat had settled into every corner of the valley so that the stones of the lane and the rock at the cave entrance radiated warmth like an oven even after the heat has been turned off. It had been too hot to wear his anorak. He'd tied the sleeves round his waist and carried it flapping over his bottom. Now he took it off and dropped it on the boulder.

"I'm back," he told the cave. He wasn't exultant but sober and determined, as if he'd made a new bargain with it.

He set about methodically laying his fire, crumpling up half the newspaper and arranging dry twigs around it in a little wigwam. When he'd done it as best he could he got out the matchbox. There were only two matches left in it. He grunted with disappointment and checked the laying of his fire again. He couldn't afford to make a mistake.

He was about to strike the match when he remembered the fish trap. He'd be a fool to light his fire before all the food was ready to cook. It would be a waste to keep it burning longer than he had to. He stowed the matchbox carefully away in the little cubby hole and ran off down to the stream. He was suddenly dying to know if his trap had worked.

He burst through the trees and jumped down onto the strip of mud by the water. Then he stopped dead. A huge grey bird, as big as a flamingo, was standing right beside the trap, its sinuous neck arched forward, the cobra hood of its head poised over the water, ready to strike.

A heron! Peter had never seen one so close before. It stood so still on its stick-like legs he could hardly believe it was real. It looked like a plastic model in a garden centre. He held his breath, not wanting to scare it.

The bird's head plummeted down into the water so fast that Peter's eyes could not follow it. It came up more slowly with a beautiful speckled trout, all of twenty-five centimetres long, in its beak.

Peter jerked back to life. It was his fish, caught in his trap! The heron was stealing it!

"Oi!" he shouted, lumbering forward. "Get out of it, you! Go on, thief! Shove off!"

The heron lifted its huge wings and rose into the air, its long legs dangling uselessly, but the fish was so heavy the bird moved in slow motion, hampered by the weight and distracted by the vigorous twitching in its beak.

"Drop it! I'll kill you! It's mine!"

Peter was dancing with fury, clapping his hands and stamping his feet. The heron was in difficulties. It was trying to hold on to the unwieldy fish, but Peter was frightening it. With a gulping lunge of its head it took a firmer grip, and rose into the air, clearing the trees.

"Thief!" roared Peter, picking up a stick and flinging it at the heron with all his might. The stick hit a branch overhead and crashed down again.

Peter burst out of the trees, back into the field. The heron had come down low again. It was flying very slowly, only a few metres above the ground. It wanted to land and find a place where it could tackle its enormous meal in peace.

Peter, chasing after it, nearly stumbled on a stone. He reached down and groped for it, keeping his eye on the heron, then took aim and threw the stone with as much precision as he could. It went wide by several feet, but the heron had had enough. It dropped the fish, which lay still twitching in the grass, then took off, hunching its neck down between its powerful shoulders and drifting through the air with effortless rotations of its vast grey wings.

The fish was a trout all right. It was brown, darker on top than underneath, with a row of speckled dots along each side. Peter picked it up cautiously, and held its slippery body in both hands, afraid it might plunge for freedom again, but the fish was at its last gasp, exhausted and dying.

There might be another, thought Peter. I haven't even looked at the trap yet.

He went back to the stream and laid the trout on the bank, pulling leaves over it in case the heron caught a gleam of its glittering body and swooped in for another try. Then, without bothering to take off his trainers, he stepped along the dry tops of the biggest stones of the dam until he came to the break in it below which the trap was set.

There was indeed another fish. It had pushed its head through two of Peter's sticks and its body was thrashing from side to side as it tried to free itself, forcing the sticks further and further apart. At any moment it would slip through and get away down the stream.

Peter squatted over it, tense with excitement, not knowing how to pick it out. If he tried grabbing it in his hands it might easily slither out of them like the first fish had done, and if he was careless he'd dislodge the wall of sticks which seemed about to collapse anyway.

If only I had a net, he thought, or my can. I could sort of scoop it up.

Then he remembered how Dad, when they had fished together in the Dordogne, had hooked his thumb and forefinger into a fish's gills. Gingerly he closed his hand round the slimy head, found the gills, tightened his grip and pulled the fish free.

"Brilliant!" he muttered. "I'm brilliant!"

He teetered back along the dry stones to the water's edge and uncovered the fish he'd rescued from the heron. The second, though not a trout, was even bigger, a good thirty centimetres long. They'd make a real, proper supper, and if the trap lasted overnight he might even find another fish ready for his breakfast as well.

{15}

Until he was back in the cave, and had put his fish down by the fireplace, Peter hadn't begun to think about how he would cook them. Apart from fish fingers they hardly ever had fish at home, except sometimes on a Saturday night, when Dad brought supper home from the fish and chip shop on the corner. That kind of fish, boneless, crusted in crisp fried batter, golden outside and white inside, had nothing in common with his two sleek trout, still with their heads and tails and their sightless dead eyes.

I could just boil them in the soup, thought Peter doubtfully, but then he realized that the can was much too small. Their tails would flop right out of it.

He suddenly remembered the man at the camp site, lifting a steak off a metal grill sitting on a bed of hot charcoal. If only he'd some kind of metal frame he could barbecue the fish. Of course! There was his wire! He could bend it in a loop or an S-shape or something, balance it on a couple of stones, and lay the fish on that. The first thing was to get the fire going. He hadn't worried about whether or not he'd be able to light it when he'd nearly tried before. He hadn't had time to think. But now he was scared. With only two matches he would have only two tries and there would be no room for mistakes.

The last time he'd made a fire, at home last autumn, when Dad had been raking up the garden rubbish and had let him do the burning, he'd used nearly half a box of matches. The newspaper had kept burning up, but the twigs had refused to catch at all, and he'd had to start all over again twice.

That stuff was wet, he told himself. This is bone dry.

Just to make sure, he carefully checked the twigs stuffed with newspaper that made up his little wigwam, fussily pushing and patting them into place and tucking in curls of paper. Then, with trembling fingers, he took a match out of the box and struck it.

The pink head of the match grated along the rough side of the box, but didn't light. He struck it again, turning it a little in case the other side worked better. Nothing happened. He was holding his breath and the palms of his hands were wet with nervous sweat. He took a firmer grip on the box and desperately hit the match against the lighting pad again. The head sheered-off and fell into the pile of kindling.

Tears splashed down his cheeks. Angrily he rubbed them away with the back of his hand and wiped his suddenly running nose on the bottom of his T-shirt. There was no point in crying. No one was there to notice or give any sympathy or help. Anyway, tears might drip on his fire and make it wet. He gulped in some air and tried to breathe normally again. He had to control himself. He still had one match left. All he could do was try again.

He took it out of the box and angled himself so that

he'd be in the right position to poke it straight into the most promising bit of his wigwam. Then, just before he struck it, he saw the head of the first match sticking out of the pile. Carefully he picked it out. There was nearly half an inch of wood left on it and the head was still sound. He dropped it back into the box, encouraged. It wasn't much of a match, but it was better than nothing. It might work if this one failed.

Finding it like that had made him feel more confident. He picked up the second match and struck it. It burst into a good strong flame. Hardly daring to breathe in case he accidently blew it out he touched his little wigwam with it. The newspaper caught. It flared up, igniting the twigs at once. The whole wigwam seemed to explode into flame.

Almost immediately, the flames began to subside.

It'll go out, thought Peter in a sudden panic.

He reached over to his pile of fuel and pulled out a couple of larger sticks. They burned up brightly. He fed the fire with more. It was fast and insatiable, eating up his supply of wood. A pile that size had lasted for hours at home, but this wood was so brittle and dry it had no staying power. It seemed to disappear at once.

I'm going to need more, masses and masses more, thought Peter anxiously. This stuff's too small and light. I need proper logs.

He built the fire up with the biggest pieces he had to make sure it had enough to feed on, then he ran outside.

The light was beginning to go now. The sun was

behind the hill and the whole valley was settling into a subdued grey dimness. He would have to work fast.

He started by looking along the ditch where he'd looked before. Nothing much was there. I've probably taken it all, he thought. He forced himself to stop and think. He had seen a few good big dead branches that had fallen from an old oak halfway towards the spring on the far side of the field. He'd had to take care stepping over them on the way back in case he spilt his water.

Without taking the time to go back to the gate, he forced his way through the hedge, then hared across the field as fast as he could.

The fallen branches were lying where he remembered them, and there were more than he'd thought. It was getting harder to see, but he could make out several excellent bits tangled up in the undergrowth. He grabbed the end of one and pulled. It came away reluctantly, held back by brambles and bindweed, its smaller twigs breaking off with satisfactorily crisp snaps. It was good and dead, and would burn beautifully. When he had pulled it right out he could see it was very long, three metres at least.

He began to break the smaller ends into manageable lengths, then he stopped. He could drag the whole thing back to the cave and break it up there. That way he would be able to take more in one journey.

He looked round again quickly to pick out other good bits. He was worried about leaving his fire any longer in case it went out. He began to pull more branches free, but the vision of cold grey ashes where his bright flames had been kept nagging at him, so he took hold of his first branch by the thickest end and began running back to the cave, stopping when he had to in order to untangle the twiggy bits at the end when they got caught in tufts of long grass.

The fire was still alight, although only just. The flames had died down, but the embers of the biggest sticks were red and glowing. Quickly he fed them with dry grass and twigs, then he blew. The flames sprang up again.

He began to relax. The fire was going to be all right now. All he had to do was break up his new fuel supply and go back for more. After that, he could get on with cooking his supper.

The trouble was, he was desperately hungry, and suddenly very tired. He wanted only to sit down and eat, then lie down by his fire and rest. The thought of going back down to the oak tree and humping a whole load of wood up to the cave irritated him and he began to feel sorry for himself again.

He knew he had no choice. If he wanted a fire, he had to fetch the fuel. If he wanted to eat cooked food, he had to cook it himself.

"Hang on a minute, Sparks," he said to the fire. "I'll be right back."

Doggedly, he set out for the tree again.

Once he'd made up his mind to build up a solid supply of fuel it took less time than he had expected. The problem was that the big logs were too heavy to carry, and the ones he could manage were too long to burn conveniently. He wished he had a proper saw, and he even opened up his Swiss army knife and took a few cuts at one of the logs with its shiny serrated blade, but it would take all night to saw just one log in half. It would be a waste of time to try.

"Yes!" he said suddenly. "Wow!" He'd had a brilliant idea. He would put the long logs right across the fire and let them burn through the middle. Then they would be cut in two pieces,and he'd be able to manage them more easily.

He piled his hoard of wood near the cave's entrance. Inside, it would take up too much space, and anyway, he was afraid a spark might accidentally set it alight. Everything here seemed to burn so easily he'd have to watch it carefully.

When he'd collected far more than he felt he could possibly need, he went back inside.

The fire had settled now into a solid, comfortable, steady speed. The flames were no longer frenzied and hungry, but had relaxed and were licking gently and lazily round the blackened pieces of wood.

"Good for you, Sparks," said Peter. "You're doing all right."

Sparks was a friend now, the best he could possibly have. Robert and Stripey were fine for daytime. They would be out sitting on their rock, he hoped, in the morning. But Sparks would be there in the night. Sparks would keep him warm and cook his food. Sparks would not take fright and run away, unless Peter failed to keep his side of the bargain, and let him run out of fuel.

The light from the fire was now almost the only light in the cave, as the daylight had all but gone. It gleamed on the smooth parts of the rock, and glimmered in the holes and corners. It threw up great black shadows which flickered and flared all around.

Good thing I explored the whole cave properly this afternoon, thought Peter. I'd have been scared stiff of the dark bits now. Especially the crevice.

As it was, he didn't particularly like the sight of its black gaping mouth, even though he knew there was nothing frightening behind it. He moved so that he was sitting with his face towards it, so he wouldn't have the uncomfortable feeling of dark emptiness behind his back. Then he picked up his length of wire and began to twist it into a grill so that he could cook his fish.

{16}

Six big queues of cars, buses and caravans were lined up on the tarmac at Calais. A robotic port official directed Billie to the longest with stiff waves of his arms. As soon as she stopped the car, Mr Castle jumped out. Billie followed suit, and leaned back against the bonnet, stretching her cramped arms while he anxiously scanned the lines of vehicles.

"Can't see Rosemary anywhere. Can you?"

"Bit difficult in this lot. They're probably over there somewhere, behind that line of coaches."

"If she's not here yet I'll have to wait. I can't go onto the ferry if she's about to miss it."

"Oh honestly, Tom, I can't see what you're so worried about. They've got their tickets and passports and everything, haven't they?"

"Yes, I suppose so. They're in the car, in the glove pocket."

"What about your passport?"

"I've got mine here." He patted his jacket pocket.

"That's all right then."

"No it isn't. Rosemary's got three kids with her. There are only two registered in her passport."

"Oh, that's OK. Sophie's got her travelcard with her in her bag. She went to Italy with my sister last year and I had to get her a proper card of her own. She refuses point blank to travel on my passport any more. She likes being independent."

"Good for her."

"Yes, and you know what, Tom, there's not a lot to be said for having your husband run off with a temp from the office, but it damn well makes you stand on your own two feet. You *and* your kids."

"I'm sure it does. If you don't mind, I'm trying to see where my car is."

"Not much point. Look at that queue over there. It's already driving onto the ship. How do we know Rosemary isn't on board already?"

"She can't be. She was behind us."

"We don't know for sure. Come on, we'd better get back in. Our queue's moving up now."

"She's going to kill me for this."

"Well, she can kill you on board. You know what I'm going to do? I'm going to go straight to the bar, and order a double gin, and drown my sorrows."

The ferry was still tantalizingly in sight when Mrs Castle pulled up at the ticket office. For the last two hours she'd driven as fast as she dared, and as the knowledge that she certainly wouldn't get to Calais in time sank in, she'd clung to the hope that the ferry would somehow be delayed. Now, seeing its huge white bulk slip serenely out through the harbour entrance into the open sea, its portholes and decks blazing with lights against the darkening sky, she dropped her head into her hands.

"What's the matter, Mum? Have we missed it?" Rachel sounded scared.

"We most certainly have."

"What'll happen to us? Will we have to sleep in the car all night?"

"I don't know. There might be another ferry later."

"But it might be full."

"Yes, Rachel, it might be full."

"Where's Daddy?"

That's exactly what I would like to know."

{17}

Peter made his grill quite easily. He looped the wire round, then made zigzags across it so that it would hold the two fish side by side without danger of them dropping through. He tried balancing them on it, longing to start cooking, but the surface of the grill was uneven and they kept slipping off. Carefully he bent the outer edges up to make a kind of cradle. It worked perfectly.

He arranged two stones, one on each side of the fire, and balanced the grill on them. Immediately, the fishes' skin began to sizzle and a marvellous smell filled the cave. He watched them anxiously. He wasn't sure how to tell when they were done.

The fire was going well, the embers a wonderful warm orange, the flames comfortably nuzzling round the sticks. As soon as he'd cooked his supper he'd lay a big oak branch across it, to start it burning through.

He took the biggest fish by the tail in order to turn it over, but it was stuck to the grill, its skin burned onto the wire. He tugged at the tail again. It came away in his hand. He poked at it with his knife, biting his lip anxiously. It might all fall to pieces, and the bits fall into the fire before he could get it free

He tried the smaller fish. It had been out of the direct flame and the skin was still intact. He eased his knife under it, snatching his hand away when the heat of the fire became too strong. When it was loose, he took the tail, which felt reassuringly firm, and flipped the fish over. He'd have to leave the bigger one on the grill, eat the underside first, then try cooking the top later if it still looked raw.

The smell was becoming unbearably delicious. Suddenly he could hold onto his hunger no longer. He lifted the grill off, holding the singeingly hot end with the sleeve of his anorak, and put it down on his sitting boulder. Then he flaked off a piece of steaming pink flesh, and put it in his mouth.

It was the most wonderful food he'd ever tasted in his whole life. He pulled off another piece. It came away less easily, and was warm rather than hot, but he was too impatient to care about whether it was cooked through or not. He put it in his mouth. It was a little raw, but not too bad, and the taste and feel of it in his mouth was still indescribably good.

"I did it, didn't I, Sparks?" he said, extracting a couple of bones from between his teeth. "I can do it. I really can."

It took him a surprisingly long time to pick each skeleton clean. He sniffed at the red, raw, spongy bits in the cavity between the walls of good pink meat, but didn't fancy it.

Next time, he thought, I'll cut them open and pull the insides out before I cook them.

He remembered how Dad had done it, slitting the

fish's belly open, pulling out the innards and throwing them to the crows.

He sat back at last and licked his fingers. There was nothing left of either fish that was remotely edible, and they'd tasted great, but although he wasn't exactly starving any more he wasn't exactly full either.

I'll do my soup now, he thought happily. He felt powerful and confident, sure he could manage anything.

He reached out for his tin can. He'd carried it back from the spring so carefully that it was still nearly full. The pile of chickweed and nettles had wilted, and looked limp and dead, but the book had said they were good to eat, and he'd have to trust it.

He picked out the best bits of chickweed and dropped them into the water. They floated about on the top. He poked them down and added some more, then gingerly picked up a nettle on the end of a stick and pushed it in. The level of water had risen almost to the surface, and there was still a huge pile of green stuff waiting to be cooked. He tipped the can over to pour some of the water out, rinsing his fishy fingers under the thin stream. It was silly to be too careful with water. He had a whole plastic bottle full, as well as what was in the can, and he could get more from the spring any time he liked.

When the can was stuffed full he carried it carefully over to the fire. The soup would be harder to cook than the fish. The can was heavy and unwieldy, and had no handle. He'd have to balance it somehow over the fire, and if it slipped and the water went everywhere it would put the fire out. He shuddered at the thought.

I'll have to get some proper cooking stones with flat tops, he thought.

He looked over towards the pile of debris under the green funnel, but it was too dark to see anything there, and he didn't want to go outside to look.

I can't leave the fire, he told himself. I can't risk it going out. He knew that wasn't the real reason. He just did not want to find out how dark it was outside.

He looked over the two stones his grill had rested on. If I'm really careful I can make it balance on them, he thought.

He pushed them around, trying to get them into a good position. Gingerly, he set his can down between them. It wobbled, and some water splashed onto the fire, which gave out a furious whoosh of smoke, leaving blackened, bone-like sticks across one whole corner. The rest of the fire seemed to shy away from the dead part, as if it was scared.

"I'm sorry, Sparks. I'm really, really, really, sorry," he said. With great care, he lifted the can off. He wouldn't risk trying again until he was quite sure it was safe.

I've just got to find more stones, he thought. He'd seen some good stones, he was sure of it, not far away, near the gate into the field. He screwed up his courage. He'd have to go outside.

It was almost completely dark now. Only the faintest greyness in the west showed where the sun had gone down. The night sky here wasn't at all like the night sky at home. There, however dark the night, there was an orange glow overhead, the reflection of the city's millions of lights. Here, the darkness was complete, broken only by a few pinprick stars. It seemed to close in, like warm, black velvet, wrapping Peter round in a sickly, soft embrace.

He felt a kind of horror shudder up from deep inside, and he nearly bolted back to Sparks and his magic circle of light and friendship. Then he remembered something Grandad had often said, before he'd had his stroke, when he was still up to organising things, and able to drive his car. "Keep cool, calm and collected."

He grabbed at the words as if they were a spell to ward off fear. Cool, calm and collected. Cool, calm and collected.

He made himself walk on. Dimly he sensed rather than saw that he was near the gate. He bent down. The faintest gleam showed up the whiteness of the stones against the grass. He felt them over with his hands, and picked one up. It seemed to have a good, smooth shape. He groped for another. It would be safer to take two.

There was a sudden beating of the air over his head, and he felt something flitter past his cheek. It frightened him so much he almost dropped the stones but he managed to hold on to them, and turned and stumbled towards the cave, gripped by a terror of the night.

He stepped into the light, dropped his stones and sank down on his heels beside the fire, his skin covered with goose bumps and the hair standing up on his arms and legs.

"Bats," he said to himself with disgust. "That's all it was. Fancy being scared of a bat!"

He fetched his stones and put them in place round the fire. They were fine. They would do just fine. He built the fire up again and balanced the can on the stones. It was perfectly steady now. He could leave it like that quite safely.

He sat back on a soft patch of sand and hugged his knees, watching for the first rising bubble, the first wisp of steam that would show him that his soup was cooking. He was trying to remember every photograph, every drawing, every film he'd ever seen of bats. He was trying to imagine the shape of their furry faces, the joints of their leathery wings, the size of their huge round ears.

I'm not afraid of bats, he thought. They can't scare me.

The soup came to the boil surprisingly quickly. He watched the whole green mass in the can rise until he was afraid it would boil over. He poked it with a stick and to his relief it subsided again.

He let it boil for a good while, in case the nettles were still able to sting, then he hooked out a green frond (it was impossible to tell if it was a nettle or some chickweed), waved it round for a moment to cool it down, and ate it.

It wasn't very nice, a bit bitter in taste, like spinach, and with some grit stuck in it, but it wasn't bad really, except that it needed salt to make it taste of anything much.

It was too difficult to think of lifting the whole can off the fire while it was so full. It was hot and heavy and could easily slip. He was scared of burning himself. He had the answer ready, though. The little can he'd brought back from the rubbish dump would make a good ladle.

He picked it up and sniffed it. It was hard to tell what had been in it originally, but it didn't smell too dirty. He poured a little water into it from the plastic bottle, and swilled it out.Then he dipped it into the soup, blew on the steaming liquid to cool it and took a sip. At least it was hot, and sort of like real food, in a way.

It took a long time to drink the soup and Peter was bored with it before he was halfway through.

At least I've had a sort of supper, he thought. I've managed. I'll do better tomorrow. I'll hunt a rabbit, and look for nuts and stuff. And I'll make a handle for my can, and get loads more wood for Sparks. Anyway, they'll come back for me tomorrow, I expect.

He didn't want to think about his family. It made him remember the dreadful, desolate feeling of being left behind. He wanted to think about Sparks instead. He wanted to look into the fire's red heart, and see caves, and staircases, and jewels.

He laid his long oak branch over the embers to start it burning through, and built round it some sturdy pieces of wood to keep it going for a good long time, then he rolled up his anorak to make a pillow, and lay down. He could go on looking at Sparks and wouldn't have to see the dark.

It wasn't very comfortable. The floor was hard and uneven. Rock dug into his thigh and shoulder and which ever way he turned something was wrong. But the fire was his comfort. He almost felt safe enough to shut his eyes, and think about going to sleep.

{18}

"You should have gone on home, Billie. There was no need for you to wait."

"Don't be daft. It was my fault we didn't wait at Calais. I might as well face Rosemary now rather than later. Anyway, I want my daughter back."

"Well, if they're not on this one, take the car and go. I'll ring you when we get home and you can come over and pick Sophie up. At least you'll get Julian into bed."

Billie laughed.

"Don't worry about him. He might as well be in bed already."

They both looked round. Julian was slumped across the back seat of the car, fast asleep.

The sonorous booming of a ship's siren resounded round Dover Dock, bouncing off the white cliffs in a series of echoes. From where they were waiting, at the exit to the port, it was impossible to see much of the incoming ferry, but Mr Castle guessed that the huge bow doors had already swung open. He could hear car engines starting up and see headlights arcing through the darkness as the first vehicles rolled down the ramp.

"Three-thirty. That's not bad. It's early. It wasn't due in for another ten minutes." He got out of the car. "You stay here, Billie, and watch for them coming through on this side. I'll go over to that corner where the headlights are likely to pick me up. She's bound to see me there if she misses you."

The first cars rolled through the customs hall and out of the dock.

"There she is! That's them! Rosemary!"

The Castles' car swung abruptly out of the stream of the traffic and pulled up sharply behind Billie's. Mrs Castle got out. She was stiff with rage. Mr Castle bit his lip, and said nothing.

"Rosemary," said Billie nervously. "I'm ever so sorry. We . . ."

Mrs Castle laughed. The sound was high-pitched and uncontrolled.

"Sorry? You're sorry? That's all right then. That makes everything all right, doesn't it? You leave me to do the whole drive on my own, get picked up by the police, get lost in Paris, damn nearly run out of petrol on the autoroute, miss the ferry, have to talk my way onto the next one – and you're sorry. Thanks, Billie. Thanks a lot."

Mr Castle stepped forward and tried to put his arms round her.

"I've been so worried about you," he said.

She pushed him off.

"Come off it, Tom. Don't give me that. You've been with Billie, haven't you? Without me. Laughing and joking. Having a great time. Just like you've been doing throughout this whole ghastly holiday."

Billie's mouth fell open. "For heaven's sake, Rosemary, you can't be jealous of me and Tom!"

"Jealous? Of course I'm not jealous. You've only been going on with each other every minute of the last two weeks. You've only been leaving me out of everything. Going off together the whole time. What have I got to be jealous about?"

"If you must know," said Billie drily, "you've got absolutely nothing to be jealous about. Especially after today. Which you would realize if you hadn't got yourself into such a state. Tom's been driving me crazy, going on and on about you all day."

"Oh, really? He was so worried, he happily went onto the ferry with you without waiting for me? I see."

"Knock it off, Rosemary. We only just caught the ferry ourselves. The cars were already driving onto it when we got to Calais. For all we knew, you were on it already."

Mrs Castle seemed to crumple.

"Oh, I see. I'm sorry. I've had such a ghastly day. I've spent the whole time thinking – imagining –"

"Yes, well," said Billie nobly, "I don't blame you. I've been a bit of a cow, I suppose. Not without a certain amount of encouragement though."

She was standing beside Mrs Castle now, and they both turned and looked reproachfully at Mr Castle.

"Here, what do you mean?" he said in a blustering voice. "What are you ganging up on me for? I tell you, I've been out of my mind all day. I kept thinking about you on the *périphérique*, and worrying about Peter being seasick. I had his pills with me in my jacket pocket. Was he sick?"

Mrs Castle looked from him to Billie and back again. "What on earth do you mean? Peter's with you!"

There was a moment's total silence.

"You mean he *isn't* with you? Oh, my God!"

"Rosemary!" Mr Castle went up to his wife, put his hands on her arms, and shook her. "Stop fooling about. Peter's with you. We've got Julian. You've got Peter and the girls."

Under the high bright street lights, Mrs Castle had looked pale. Now she looked deathly.

"I haven't got him!" she said, her voice high-pitched and shrill again. "I called out to you when we were leaving that picnic place. 'Have you got Peter?' I said."

"No, you didn't. You said, 'Have you got petrol?'"

"Oh God! Oh, my God!" Mrs Castle was shaking uncontrollably. She staggered back and held onto the roof of the car for support. "We've left him behind! He's back at that picnic place! Oh, I shall never forgive myself. Anything might have happened to him by now. He might have been picked up by someone. He might . . ."

"Stop it," said Mr Castle roughly. "Chances are he's sitting in some French farmhouse right now, being spoiled rotten by the farmer's wife. Check your mobile. I bet he's already texted us."

"Texted us? How? His mobile's in the car."

Mr Castle bit his lip.

"I'll inform the authorities at once," he said. "I'll tell them where he is. They'll get the French police onto it and pick him up."

"Yes," said Mrs Castle, "but where is he?"

"At the picnic place, of course, where we . . ." He stopped.

"Exactly, Tom. We don't know where it was, do we?"

"Here," said Mr Castle, anxiety making him sound angry. "Where's the map, for heaven's sake? We must be able to find it."

Billie dived into her car and pulled out a big road atlas.

"Put your headlights on," said Mr Castle, and he went to the front of the car and held the book open in the light.

"It was before Moulins, anyway."

"No, it wasn't." Mrs Castle was breathing with difficulty. "I remember the sign to Moulins before we turned off. At least, I think I do."

"We can't waste any more time fooling around with maps," said Mr Castle, snapping the book shut. "I'm going straight to the police."

"Mum!" Sophie had wound down her window. "Hello, Mum. Can't we go home? I'm tired."

"Just a minute, love." Billie stepped into the beam of light. "Look, Rosemary, why don't I take the kids home now in my car? Rachel can come and stay the night with us. It'll leave you freer to sort things out."

Mrs Castle seemed to have difficulty taking in what Billie had said. Mr Castle nodded.

"Good idea. Thanks." He put his arm round Mrs Castle's shoulders. This time she didn't resist."Why don't you go back with Billie, darling? You're completely exhausted. I'll deal with this."

"What are you going to do?" Mrs Castle moved her head slowly as if she was sleepwalking, as if she'd been stunned.

"I'm going to get the police here to contact Interpol in France. Then I'm taking the next ferry back to Calais, and I'm going to drive back along the way we came and see if I can find the place myself."

Mrs Castle seemed to wake up.

"Right," she said. "You take Rachel, Billie. Tom, I'm coming with you."

{19}

Peter was crammed onto a narrow ledge which sloped down towards a terrible abyss. Hornets were buzzing round his face and a heron was pecking at his hands, trying to dislodge them from the crumbling rocks they were clinging to. Tied to his belt was a tin can which dug painfully into his hip, but he knew he must not let it go. If he did he'd fall down and down and down.

Someone was calling him.

"Where are you-ou?"

He turned his head away. It was Dad's voice, but he didn't want to see Dad. Dad was with Billie, laughing and whispering. They were coming towards him. They hadn't noticed him. They were going to push him off the ledge. He moved to get out of their way, and the tin bit into him as if it was cutting his thigh open. He rolled over to ease the pain, and just as he plunged over the edge of the cliff, he woke up.

It was a moment or two before the dream left him. He felt along his thigh. The pain was real, but there was no can. Instead there was a sharp bump in the rock floor on which he'd been lying. There were no hornets either, only the infuriating whine of a mosquito hovering round his left ear. And no one was calling him. All he could hear was the hooting of an owl.

The ledge, the abyss and the blue sky above faded away, and as he woke more fully he remembered where he was and how he'd come to be there.

He shivered. It wasn't cold exactly, but he was used to sleeping with something over him, even on the hottest night, and it wasn't hot now in the cave. Then he remembered Sparks, and sat up. There was no light at all coming from the fireplace and no warmth either. The fire had gone out.

It was as if he'd been abandoned all over again. Misery engulfed him. He felt stiff and bruised, and his skin was uncomfortably dry and itchy with grit. He hugged his knees, angry with the fire for going out, angry with Dad and Mum, furious with Billie and the whole world.

Then he saw something move. The only light in the cave was a faint radiance at its mouth, just strong enough to cast a few shadows. He could interpret most of them. He knew which bumps in the rock wall and bunches of foliage hanging down over the entrance had made them. But this shadow was a stranger. It was enormously tall and thin. It seemed to creep along the wall like a huge, emaciated stick man, advancing and beckoning with clawed fingers, then retreating again on mocking tiptoes.

Peter felt the hair on his head stand on end. He sat perfectly still. He was wide awake now, alert to every creak, every rustle, every hint of movement outside and inside the cave. Everything threatened him. Everything frightened him. He buried his head in his arms. He could no longer look at the stick man on the wall. He knew it would come for him if he did. It would cross the cave on its horrible spindly legs and touch him with its ghostly fingers, and he would look into its empty eyes.

His mouth was dry. He felt the weight of fear pressing down on his shoulders.

Keep cool, calm and collected, he told himself.

The words were useless now. He needed something more powerful. It was no good trying to be cool, calm and collected all on his own. The terror was too strong.

He'd stayed with Grandad and Grandma by himself when he was very small, when Rachel was being born. He'd been frightened in the night, waking up in a strange bed, and had started crying. Grandad had heard him and come in, padding across the floor in his old bedroom slippers, his dressing-gown giving out wafts of tobacco and hair oil as it flapped round his pyjama legs.

Grandad had knelt down beside Peter's bed and put his arms round him. He'd stayed for a long time, cheering him up, and chatting, and then he'd said a prayer. It was something about angels. "Four angels round my bed," was all Peter could remember.

Grandad had abandoned Peter too. He'd gone back to bed, and a few years later he'd died had gone forever. But after he'd left the room that night, Peter had felt good. He'd snuggled down in bed and imagined the angels all round him.

He tried to think of angels now. The trouble was, he didn't believe in them. They disappeared at the touch of his thought. They weren't real, like the stick man on the wall.

A sudden despairing scream, coming from above the green funnel, made Peter flinch and tighten every muscle. That was real enough. If it had come from a ghost, it was a real ghost. If it had come from a murder victim, the body had flesh and bones.

Peter had a wild desire to bolt, to run and run until he dropped, to escape from the ledge and the abyss, the stick man and the murderer, but although he was wound up like a steel spring ready to fly open and leap up at the merest touch, he held himself down.

He racked his brains to remember a prayer.

Our Father who art in heaven. He couldn't remember any more.

Four angels round my bed. He couldn't recapture the safeness, the comfort, the warmth of Grandad's arms.

Please look after me, God. Keep me safe.

He couldn't imagine God, but his breathing was steadying down again.

You're supposed to pray with your eyes shut, he thought. He could understand why now. With his eyes screwed up tight and buried in his knees he couldn't see the stick man. Instead he could see himself, as if from above, and round him, forming all around him, was a kind of barrier, an invisible force field. The stick man and the screaming and the darkness prowled outside it, but if he concentrated he could keep them at bay.

He would go for the stick man first. He would think

him to death. He would name his fears, as he'd named the hornet, and nail them one by one.

He opened his eyes and dared to look at the stick man again. He was beckoning and retreating, beckoning and retreating in an endless, silly dance.

Clawfingers, thought Peter. Claws. Get stuffed, Claws, You can't get off that wall. You're stuck there for ever.

He felt triumphant. He even had enough courage to crawl a few feet towards Claws to look at him more closely.

He nearly laughed aloud. Claws was no more than the shadow of a dead thorn branch, swaying in the breeze outside the cave, through which the pale light of a three-quarter moon was shining.

Peter could stand up now and look outside. The moon was well risen and its light had beaten off the deep, choking darkness. He could see the lane stretching away in either direction, and the trees across the field by the stream. The moonlight was calming him. He felt bolder.

Then he heard the screaming again. It came from near at hand, and there were other sounds too, scufflings, and a kind of dry, high-pitched, barking cough. Fear attacked him again, sapping his courage. There was something out there, something evil, which was trying to catch him.

The name, he thought. Think of its name.

A dark shape was moving along the lane, low to the ground and furtive. Peter stepped back on silent feet, hardly bearing to watch but unable to look away. The thing came closer. It was trotting on four jerky feet. It was nearly at the cave.

A fox! It was only a fox carrying something in its mouth, a rabbit or a hare. It stopped for a long moment opposite the cave entrance, and turned to look inside, the furry prey dangling limp and lifeless from its jaws. For a moment it stared straight into Peter's eyes, then it turned aside towards the hedge and disappeared through a gap into the field.

Only a fox, thought Peter again. And the screaming must have been the rabbit. Fox the Jawman. Claws and Jawman. They can get lost, they can.

Suddenly he felt extremely tired. He looked at his watch. Two-thirty. He was disappointed. There were still hours to go till dawn. He'd thought the night was nearly over.

He went back to his sleeping place, but stumbled and kicked against one end of the log that he'd set on the fire to burn through. It rolled over and a piece of charred wood, coated in white ash, fell off. Under it was a faint glow of red.

"Sparks!" said Peter out loud. "You're still alive!"

He felt his way to his pile of kindling, pulled out a few likely shaped twigs, laid them across the glowing ember and blew. The dull red glowed orange, then brilliant yellow as a twig burst into flame. In the light of the fire, the moonlight faded to nothing, and the stick man disappeared. Feverishly, Peter retrieved the half-burnt ends of the old logs and fed the flames, then he built them up to a crackling blaze with kindling from his pile.

"I've killed you, Claws," he said with satisfaction. "You're dead."

The flames were warming him, comforting and strengthening him as they had done before. He could lie down again now. The two ends of oak were crossed over each other. They would easily last until morning.

"Good night, Robert. Good night, Stripey," whispered Peter. "Good hunting, Jawman. Fade out and die, Claws."

The fire was his protection now, but with it there was something else. As he shut his eyes on the dancing flames, he saw in his mind's eye another brightness. Four angels were shaping a covered nest with their wings and he was lying in it. Strong, soft feathers were above and below, all around him, and they were carrying him off in a swooping, glorious flight through the conquered darkness.

{20}

Mrs Castle couldn't take her eyes off the second hand as it blipped round the face of the clock, high up on the cream painted wall. Time seemed to be racing on, precious minutes ticking past in this stuffy little room, while Peter was lost and alone or maybe even in danger.

The pale, middle-aged policeman, who looked less than impressive without his cap, seemed to be taking hours to write down the simplest things. Name, age, address, colour of hair, colour of eyes, height, build – surely he could be doing it faster?

"Any special identifying marks?" he asked. "Scars, birthmarks et cetera?"

A horrible picture came into Mrs Castle's mind of Peter being found dead, and a foreign policeman ticking scars and birthmarks off on a list as he checked over the white, cold body. She groped in her pocket for her handkerchief. Mr Castle tried to take her hand. She pushed his away.

"This is all your fault," she whispered savagely. "If you hadn't been so . . ."

Mr Castle looked embarrassed.

"Don't go over all that again, Rosemary. I've said I'm sorry."

"Does he wear glasses?" the policeman interrupted. He hadn't raised his eyes from his notebook. "Can you describe his clothing?"

"We told the man on the desk all that before, when we first came in," burst out Mrs Castle."Can't you hurry up? We've been here half-an-hour. It's nearly a quarter-to-five already."

The policeman went on writing with maddening deliberation. He was used to emotional outbursts. He found it easiest to ignore them.

"Not much we can do at the moment anyway," he said, "until we've managed to contact the European Liaison Unit. It's a bit difficult at this time of day. They're short-staffed."

"Short-staffed? *Short-staffed*? There's a kid lost in the middle of France and you tell me you're short-staffed?"

The door opened, and an older policeman came in, with a tray of teacups.

"Liquid refreshment," he said breezily. "You look as if you need it."

Mrs Castle turned to him eagerly.

"Anything happened?"

"The European Liaison Unit are going to phone us back in the next half-hour. They'll take all the details then. It'll probably go through Interpol and the French police after that."

Mrs Castle let out a sob.

"Come on Rosemary, cheer up," said Mr Castle, his own forehead furrowed with anxiety. "They'll put out a radio appeal I expect. Get it on TV. We'll have the whole of France looking for him."

The older policeman silently set a cup of tea down in front of Mr Castle, and went out of the room.

"I wouldn't bank on much publicity, sir," the pale one said. "Peter's not likely to get any press coverge. No suspicious circumstances, if you know what I mean. There's hundreds of kids go missing all over Europe every day. You can't put them all on TV."

"What'll they do? How will they find him?" wailed Mrs Castle.

"They'll circulate the local force with his details, most probably, and start making enquiries in the area where he was last seen. They might even get a local radio station to issue a description. You never know your luck."

"But all that could take weeks!"

"They'll act at once. Very efficient, the French police are. Anyway, if he's a sensible lad, like you say he is, he'll have contacted someone himself by now. He's probably in police custody already."

Mr Castle pushed his teacup away. He hadn't touched it.

"If he isn't, we'll probably find him before the French police do."

The pale policeman put two teaspoons of sugar into his thick china cup and stirred the almost orange tea.

"I wouldn't advise that, sir. We wouldn't recommend your rushing over there to make enquiries on your own behalf."

"What do you mean? Why not? He's our son, isn't he?"

"Of course, you're entitled to take that action if you

so wish, but we will require a contact person at this end. We'll have to be able to get hold of someone responsible if there's a need to act on information received from the French end."

"You mean you want us to go home, and sit twiddling our thumbs, waiting for the telephone to ring while the French police might or might not bother to make a proper search for our son? Forget it, chum. We're going back to Calais on the next ferry."

"I think you'll find it best in the long run to follow the established procedure, Mr Castle. We will require you, for example, to supply a recent photograph of your son."

"He's got a point there, Tom," said Mrs Castle doubtfully.

"Also," went on the policeman, "if, as is most likely, Peter has already been picked up, someone will need to be at the address he'll supply to the French police so that we can be apprised of the fact that he is found."

Mrs Castle had another dreadful vision, of the phone ringing and ringing in the empty house, while Peter sat in despair, waiting for someone to answer it.

She picked up her handbag, ready to jump up and start for home at once.

"He's right," she said. "You'd better go back by yourself Tom. I'll go home straight away. Peter doesn't know my mobile number off by heart. Only the home one. The phone's probably ringing right now for all we know. It'll only take a couple of hours to get there at this time of night. The roads will be practically empty."

"Hang on a minute, Rosemary." Mr Castle was feeling through his pockets for his own set of keys. "I'll have to take the car, remember?"

"Really, Mr Castle, I wouldn't . . ."

Mr Castle ignored the policeman. He went on talking to his wife.

"Come to think of it, I'll drive you home, just in case Peter's phoned, and if he hasn't I'll pick up a photo of him. We should be there by seven if we leave now. You can stay by the phone, and I'll get back here in time for the ten o'clock ferry. I'll be back down in the right part of France by late afternoon, and I'll keep phoning back to check with you. I'll retrace our journey. I'm sure I'll recognise the place where we left the road."

He stood up and picked up his jacket. The policeman shook his head.

"I'm afraid I must ask you to remain here, Mr Castle, at least until such time as the European Liaison Unit gets back to us. You may be required to supply further information. I'm sure you would wish to be as cooperative as possible. The more you can tell us about Peter the easier it will be to find him. A lot may depend on it."

Mr Castle groaned and sat down again. The policeman smiled sympathetically.

"I know, sir. Very frustrating. Still, you know what they say, 'They also serve who only stand and wait.' Now, where were we? Oh yes. What make of trainers was he wearing?"

{21}

In spite of the good, safe feeling Peter had had before he went to sleep for the second time, he slept badly, jerking awake at every sound from outside. It was surprising how many noises there were, even in the dead of night; rustlings and hootings and the terrifying, unearthly screech of some huge owl-like bird that flew between him and the moon before it set, swollen to a great white disc, over the horizon.

He wriggled and turned dozens of times, trying to make himself comfortable, but as the night wore on the rock seemed to get harder and the pockets in it grittier. He was bruised all over, and itchy too. He needed his anorak for a pillow, but if he bundled it up and put it under his head he felt chilly. He kept changing it round, unable to decide which way was the least awful.

Eventually, he opened his eyes to find that the sky was beginning to go grey. Claws had long since disappeared, slipping out of the cave as the moon had gone down, and Peter's fear had vanished with him. He wasn't scared now, just lonely, and sorry for himself.

The dawn light was cold and unfriendly. Worst of all, the fire had gone out again, and though Peter stirred the charred stumps there was no hint of warmth left in it. He shut his eyes, trying to sink back into sleep in order to put off the effort of starting the day, but he could only doze, and everytime he opened his eyes again the light was stronger and the chorus of bird song louder.

At last the paleness in the sky turned to a lurid orange. Peter gave up trying to sleep. He sat up, stretching his stiff limbs one by one, then he staggered to his feet and went outside.

The circle of orange on the horizon was deepening in intensity. It was striped across with a couple of thin purple clouds which disappeared as the edge of the sun, like a burning saucer, popped up over the hill. It was too bright to watch any longer, but he could feel its marvellous warmth on his face.

Overhead he became aware of an eerie, mewing sound. A huge brown bird, a buzzard or a kite, was slowly batting its wings against the morning air.

He belongs here, thought Peter. This is all home to him.

He felt lonelier than ever. Home for him was 16, St David's Road. Home had comfortable armchairs, and a TV, and a bathroom, and his own bedroom with his things in it. He couldn't believe how easily home could be lost.

The buzzard landed on a tree, settling its wings in slow motion along its broad brown sides.

"You're lucky," said Peter out loud. "You don't need a house or anything. You've only got to choose a perch when you go to bed, without any pillows or sheets or stuff like that."

He looked back into the cave. It was different this morning. Yesterday afternoon it had been mysterious, a cool, fun place in which to dream and plan. While Sparks was alive it had been a haven, secure and comforting against the wicked darkness. When Claws tiptoed in, horror had come with him. The rock walls had been full of terror, which had tried to take over his mind. But now the cave was nothing more than a hole in the side of the hill, bare, dusty and uncomfortable.

They'll come back for me today, thought Peter. Before tonight, anyway. They must.

The idea of the day stretching ahead made him think of food. He had a gnawing, nagging hunger, worse than yesterday's. He'd have to find something to eat for breakfast, and then he'd have to think of lunch, and maybe supper too. He went back inside and took a swig out of his plastic bottle. The spring water still tasted good, and made him feel more cheerful. He hadn't realized how thirsty he had been.

The only problem was, he couldn't imagine living on water. He couldn't bear the thought of being permanently hungry.

The idea of more fish wasn't particularly appealing but he could at least go and see if his trap had caught anything overnight. He set off, running across the field. The dew was heavy and his trainers were soon soaked, but the sun was already so hot it didn't seem to matter.

He was nearly at the stream when the deep silence of

the valley was broken by the distant hum of a tractor. It was visible already, coming along the lane from the direction of the camp site, chugging very slowly behind a herd of milky white cows.

It's probably the man with the scar, Peter thought doubtfully. Looks like the same tractor, anyway.

He slipped into the cover of the undergrowth by the stream. It was too late to get safely across the lane and back into the cave. He would be seen.

At the gate into the field the tractor stopped and the driver climbed out. Peter recognised his checked shirt and flat cap. It was Scarface all right, no doubt about that. Peter was glad he'd wriggled through the hedge and hadn't undone the gate. He didn't like the idea of a suspicious Scarface wondering who had left it open, and hunting round, and catching him.

The farmer opened the gate and drove into the field, followed by his herd. Peter watched with relief as the soft plump cows fanned out across the wet grass. His own tell-tale footprints in the dew were quickly being obliterated.

He waited for the farmer to back the tractor out into the lane again, but saw instead that he was closing the gate behind him. Now he was back in the tractor cab, and was driving right down to the stream, coming straight for the tree behind which Peter was hiding.

Peter couldn't move. His brain was ordering him to step out, go up to the farmer, and ask for help, but his instincts screamed at him to stay hidden.

The tractor came on. It was nearly in the water now. Peter waited for it to stop, but instead the farmer revved the engine, ploughed straight into the stream, where it ran over a kind of ford, formed by a layer of smooth flat stones, and roared up the bank on the other side.

Peter let out his breath. He was relieved, but disappointed too. The tractor would soon be up at the top of the hill. It would disappear over the horizon, and he'd be alone in the valley again, with no other human being in sight. But the tractor stopped. The man jumped down once more and strode back to the stream. He'd seen the dam and the fish trap.

He walked up and down the bank, looking at the whole construction, scowling and muttering to himself. Then he picked up a stick, and with a few swipes demolished both trap and dam. The stream reverted to its old channel at once, and in a few seconds it was as if the dam had never been there at all.

Peter watched helplessly, angry now rather than scared. His dam, his trap and his breakfast were being destroyed before his eyes. He wanted to run out and shout at the man, tell him what he thought of him, beat him with his own stick. Furious tears were splashing down his cheeks.

Then he remembered the Dordogne, and the business of fishing permits. Dad had had to go along to see the local farmer and pay something for a licence before they'd been allowed to fish in the river. Perhaps it was the same here. If so, he'd broken the law catching those fish last night. He'd been poaching. Poaching was a criminal act, he knew that much. You could be put into prison for poaching in some countries. If they catch me now, he thought, and take me away for poaching, Dad'll never find me.

Anxiety had chased away his anger. He watched the tractor rumble away up the hill, and walked thoughtfully up along the hedgerow, stopping to pick more blackberries on the way. This time the noisy chattering of a squirrel led him to a scrubby tree, sticking up out of the hedge, on which grew handfuls of hazel-nuts. He picked a good lot, and stuffed them into his pockets. They were still unripe, the shells quite soft, and the kernels green, but he cracked a few of them and ate them as he walked along. They tasted good enough.

The sun was slanting into the cave now, lighting up the remains of his fire, and his cans and bottle. Anyone looking in could easily see that someone had made a fire and cooked over it.

Can't risk that, Peter thought. He scattered the ashes and carried the half-burnt logs to his fuel pile, covering them with unburnt pieces of wood. With the charred ends hidden, the mass of dead sticks looked natural, as if they'd fallen down the green funnel on their own. Then he pushed his cans and bottle into the crevice. They could only be seen if someone lay right down to look in, and then they only looked like rubbish, abandoned by campers or picnickers.

When he'd finished, the cave looked almost the same

as it had been yesterday, before he'd found it, anonymous, waiting, uninhabited except for two lizards, a dull brown one and a brilliantly striped green and silver one, who were sunning themselves on a rock at the entrance.

"Hello, you guys," said Peter. "Look after the place while I'm out."

He tied the sleeves of his anorak round his waist, checked that his knife was in his pocket and picked up his length of wire.

He'd go up to the spinney above the cave to explore. The scream from the rabbit the fox had caught in the night had come from somewhere up there. If he found a likely looking hole he'd make a noose to put over it, and catch a bunny for himself. He'd studied the pictures in his survival book often enough. He was sure he knew how it could be done.

He left the cave and scrambled through the fence into the field behind it. The going was easier once he was past the bushes that grew thickly above the green tunnel.

He stopped every now and then to look round, anxious to keep watch behind his back, in case there was anyone around to see him. Halfway up to the spinney, he had to drop down on his hands and knees, into the long tussocky grass. The boy from the camp site was trotting purposefully down the lane, looking about as if he was searching for something.

"Don't you go into my cave," Peter muttered under his breath. "Don't you dare."

The boy stopped at the mouth of the cave and looked

in. He hesitated for a moment, but didn't go inside. Then he turned round, and set off back towards the camp site.

Peter let out the long breath he'd been holding. He felt exultant. He'd covered his traces well. He felt as if he'd passed a test. He watched the boy's disappearing back almost approvingly.

No need to be afraid of him anyway, he thought. He's years younger than me. At least a year, anyway.

He waited until the boy was out of sight, then he went on up towards the spinney.

{22}

In the small bedroom of Gendarme Chassot's flat above the Gendarmerie, just outside the centre of St Didier-les-Bois, the alarm bell suddenly shrilled out, waking him, his wife and the baby, who started crying at once.

"Damn," muttered Chassot. He rolled over and groped for his watch, knocking over the lamp with its pink frilled shade on the marble-topped bedside table.

Five-thirty. That wasn't so bad. Nearly time to get up anyway. He went over to the cot, picked up his little daughter and took her over to his wife. She sat herself up against the peachy flowered pillows and pulled open the buttons of her nightdress, yawning as she did so. The baby nuzzled into her full breast and began to drink noisily.

Gendarme Chassot pulled on his blue uniform trousers and short sleeved shirt. It was warm already. It would be another scorcher today.

By the time he'd got down to the office the message had finished printing itself out on the computer in the little communications room. He tore it off. It was probably just another fuss from the gendarme military headquarters in Vichy. The colonel was a new broom trying to sweep the whole Company clean.

He read the message, and swore again, this time more

loudly. A lost child, no clear whereabouts, missing for over fifteen hours already and foreign too. It was just what he needed on a hot Sunday, when he'd hoped for a quiet day to recover from the big dinner last night. Anyway, he hated this business of missing children. You hunted with increasing urgency as time went by, but you dreaded what you might find. Now that he had a baby of his own, the thought of a lost child made him feel sick in a way it had never done before.

The description of the boy was clear enough – brown straight hair, brown eyes, height 1.20m, buff coloured shorts, green T-shirt, old marked white trainers – but the area of search was huge. The operation would be massive. Gendarmes all over the Auvergne must have been wrenched out of bed and be scratching their heads and longing for their morning cup of coffee just like he was.

He grinned sourly at the thought, then read the message again. There was one significant clue. *Missing minor last seen in vicinity caves and stream.*

He made a rapid mental scan of the district. There were caves over at Villefranche and La Forêt, and then old Favier, the farmer just near St Didier up on the hill had a cave somewhere on his land.

Behind him on the wall was a list of essential phone numbers, the mayors of the twelve local communes, the fire brigade, the doctors, the judges. According to the rule book he had to contact the mayors first. Most of them were retired old boys, who would still be asleep in bed at this hour. There would be a great deal of huffing and puffing as the sacred peace of their Sunday morning was shattered.

He sat down at his desk, pulled the phone towards him, and punched in the first number. He'd start with Monsieur Gérard, the most experienced of all the local mayors. What he didn't know about the surrounding villages and the doings of their inhabitants was not worth knowing.

". . . and over the central region another very hot day, with a possibility of clouds moving in from the west towards evening. Temperatures will remain . . ."

The telephone rang. Madame Favier dusted her flowery hands quickly on her apron and picked up the receiver.

"Hello, Maurice. No, Roland's still out seeing to the cows. What? Oh, another half-hour I should think. Do you want him to ring you when he comes in? Is it urgent?"

She listened for a while as Maurice Gérard's voice crackled down the wire, her hand tightly gripping the receiver. She had long since given up hope of having another child of her own, to replace little Phillippe, who had died years ago, and nothing in the world upset and angered her more than reports of children who had been neglected or abandoned by callous parents or molested by crazy perverts.

From outside came the clanking roar of the tractor turning into the farmyard.

"Here he is now," Madame Favier said down the phone. "No, don't worry Maurice, I'll tell him. We'll go and take a look down by the caves straight away."

She put the receiver down and ran outside. It had been cool and dim inside the ancient, thick-walled farmhouse kitchen, and she had to put her hand up to shade her eyes in order to see her husband.

"Don't put the tractor away, Roland!" she shouted across to him. "We've got to get going straight away. Maurice Gérard's just called. There's a little English boy missing somewhere round here, and the last place he was seen in was a cave."

{23}

The wood above the cave was fenced with close set lines of barbed wire, and Peter tore his T-shirt as he wriggled underneath it.

The grass in the field had been heavy with dew, but the ground was dry under the close growing trees. There were very few tall, thick trunks. Most were spindly with several narrow stems shooting up from the same spot. The wood was so quiet that every movement Peter made seemed unnaturally loud. Even the slight swishing sound of dead leaves stirred by his feet seemed to carry a long way. The air was still, and there was no breeze to rustle the leaves. The birds, too, seemed to have fallen silent, though he could hear the mournful cawing of crows, some distance away.

He didn't like the wood. It felt dead and stuffy, too hot even at this early hour of the day. He went forward uncertainly. He couldn't imagine finding anything to eat in here, and that was all he cared about now. Yesterday, he'd have looked out for possible trees to climb, and good bits of wood to build a base with. Yesterday felt like years ago.

Suddenly he stopped. On the bare earth in front of him was something long, straight and bright orange. He bent down to take a closer look and jumped back in disgust. The thing was a giant slug, a good ten centimetres long, its antennae extended, its grooved back rippling as it slid along.

They probably used to eat those in the Stone Age, he thought. He nearly retched at the idea. The funny thing was he had quite liked snails, when they'd all tried them for fun, last week, down in the Dordogne.

"Slugs are only snails without shells," he told himself reasonably. "I suppose, if I got hungry enough . . . "

Then another thought occured to him. He'd heard somewhere that brightly coloured insects and reptiles were usually poisonous. This slug could be deadly, as far as he knew. He wouldn't, after all, have to put himself to the test.

The wood was getting him down. He wanted to get out at once. He ran on up the hill, weaving between the trees, to the place where he could see most daylight coming through the trunks. He emerged higher up in the same field from which he'd entered the wood.

He was halfway to the top of the hill now, and had a good view of the whole valley, with the lane and the stream running along the bottom of it. There were the cows, scattered about on the yellowing August grass, there was the rocky outcrop above the spring, and there was the camp site, half hidden in the trees. But what caught his eye was the sight of a ridged, red-tiled roof, peeping out from over the top of the hillside on the opposite side of the valley. It was from that direction that the tractor and the cows had come this morning. There was probably a farm up there, old Scarface's farm, perhaps.

He went further up the hill to get a better view. It was a farm all right. The roof he'd seen first clearly belonged to a big barn, and next to it was an old farmhouse, a nice looking place, the sort of house small children draw, with a front door in the middle, and a window on each side, and a flower bed with brightly coloured flowers along the front wall.

Now he could hear the tractor starting up. It wasn't coming from the farm, but over to the right, from the direction of the camp site. It must have gone round that way in a loop from the farm, and have stopped there for a while. Here it came now, out from behind the clump of trees, making for the cave.

Peter stepped back into the shelter of the branches overhanging the field from the edge of the wood, and watched. There were two people on the tractor, the driver, and a passenger, a woman, riding awkwardly on the wing.

The tractor stopped beside the cave, and the man, Scarface, helped the woman down. Peter couldn't see her clearly, but she looked middle-aged, older than Mum, anyway, and she was wearing a navy blue print dress, with short sleeves. Her arms were plump, and her waist thick.

They both disappeared into the cave. A few moments later, they came out and the man stood with his hands shading his eyes, scanning the fields and hillsides in all directions. The woman wandered up the lane, looking along the ditch and by the hedge.

Peter kept perfectly still. He was confident that the man, with the sun in his eyes, wouldn't be able to see him unless he attracted attention by moving.

He was right. Scarface dropped his hand and went down to the stream. He stayed there for a while, and every now and then Peter caught sight of his brightly coloured shirt between overhanging trees. He emerged slowly, looking round him all the time, and came back across the field, called to the woman, and they both climbed onto the tractor.

They're looking for the person who made the trap, thought Peter. They're looking for me. He felt his flesh creep, and shivered, in spite of the heat. This was how an animal must feel when it was being hunted, how the rabbit had felt before it died in the fox's relentless teeth.

Rabbits. He'd come up here to look for rabbits. The tractor was disappearing now, back down the lane where it had come from. It was safe to step out from the shelter of the trees.

As he did so he saw a sudden flash of white from along the edge of the wood, further down the hill. It was a rabbit! Its white scut was disappearing down a hole among the roots of one of the few large old trees that bordered the field at the edge of the wood. This was where Jawman must have been last night. The rabbit's scream had come from here.

He'd been lucky. If the farmer hadn't come along, he wouldn't have hidden himself and kept still, and the rabbit would have stayed in its burrow. He would never have seen it.

He sat down and began to work at his length of wire. He'd imagined making traps hundreds of times. In his mind's eye he'd visualised clever systems of levers and springs and counterweights. But now that he needed to make a real one, to catch a real animal, his ideas seemed stupid and unrealistic. He would try to do something simple, but effective.

He would make a loop out of his wire, secure the end with a simple twist so that it would tighten automatically when he pulled it, place it over the rabbit hole, and wait. When the rabbit came out to feed again, as it would if he kept still and quiet enough, he would twitch the wire, and it would tighten round the rabbit. He'd swing it up, and the rabbit would be his, dangling from the wire the way the other one had dangled from the fox's jaws. All he had to do was keep far enough away, so that the rabbit wouldn't be alarmed by his scent.

It was quite easy to make the wire into a noose. Peter checked it a couple of times on his arm. It slid tight easily, and bit into his arm without coming undone however hard he tugged it. It should easily be strong enough to hold a rabbit.

When it was ready he tiptoed over the grass, hoping to minimize the vibrations of his footsteps, which the rabbit might sense underground, and quickly and quietly arranged the noose over the hole. Then he crept backwards away from it, as far as the wire would let him, and sat down in the grass to watch and wait.

Nothing happened. A spider ran up his leg. He shook it off with the smallest possible movement. His head started itching. When he could bear it no longer, he gingerly lifted his hand to scratch it.

It was much harder than he'd imagined to keep his eyes fixed on one place all the time. He heard a rustle in the wood behind him, and wanted badly to look round and see what was making it. He resisted the temptation.

Then suddenly he realized that he had looked away. He'd allowed his eyes to follow the jerky flight of a small blue butterfly. He'd been watching it for quite a while as it settled first on one small field flower, then on another, opening and closing its sky-coloured wings in the sun.

He turned his head with the slowest of movements, back towards the rabbit hole. He nearly jerked the wire in his excitement, but stopped himself just in time. A pair of long brown ears was sticking up out of the hole, moving round like radar sensors to pick up the slightest sound. He could just see a twitching black nose, delicately sniffing, the whiskers beside it spraying out, alert as an insect's antennae. It seemed to know that something was wrong.

Perhaps the wire smells funny, Peter thought.

He'd never been so close to a wild rabbit before, though he'd stroked and held his class's rabbit dozens of times when he'd been at his old school. This creature was as unlike that lazy, soft, contented thing as a pet dog was from a wolf. This rabbit was alive in every nerve, lean, fit, timid, unsure of what to do.

The first rabbit he'd ever known suddenly popped into his head. It had been a picture on a mug which someone had given him for his first birthday. The rabbit had been wearing a little blue coat, and was being chased out of a vegetable garden by an angry old man.

Peter tried to blot the picture out. He mustn't remember that rabbit's name. He had to think about this one. He had to kill it, strangle it in his noose, bash it over its head with a stone to finish it off, rip off its fur with his knife, cook its meat over a fire, stuff it into his mouth, chew it and swallow it. But the name printed on his mug was forcing itself into his mind. He couldn't push it out.

"Peter," he muttered helplessly. "Peter Rabbit."

The wild creature, reassured by the stillness and silence all round, began to move cautiously up out of its hole. It was inside the noose now. Peter only had to pull, and the wire would tighten round its soft, trembling body.

Peter dropped his end of the wire, jumped up and waved his arms.

"Go back in, you fool! Oh, you stupid *fool*, can't you be more careful?"

The rabbit had disappeared before he'd finished shouting the first word. Peter stood still and looked helplessly at its empty hole, the wire dangling limp and useless from his hand.

{24}

Stéphane Bourlaud was enjoying an extremely interesting morning. These annual camping holidays were a mixed blessing as far as he was concerned. The biggest advantage was in getting away from the block of flats in the rue Stalingrad in Moulins. For a few weeks he could live without the constant terror of being ambushed by the Durand gang, who haunted the end of the street near the baker's (which he had to pass whenever he wanted to go anywhere), and who would attack him for no reason, insulting him, punching him and rolling him in the dirt.

The other reason why he liked being here was the fun he had exploring on his own. He wasn't like his brother, Jean-Pierre, who was always in the middle of a gang of mates, always looking for trouble, ready to take on anyone who got in his way. Stéphane was a loner, an observer. He was good at watching and listening.

Monsieur Bourlaud spent his holiday practising his poaching techniques, illicitly fishing for trout and trapping small prey, enjoying a game of hide and seek with the local farmers. Stéphane admired his skill and daring. He longed to be taken out on poaching expeditions. He wanted his father to teach him how to set a trap and cast a fly. Once or twice he'd almost dared to ask, but he wasn't in the habit of talking to his father, and dread of Monsieur Bourlaud's violent temper held him back.

Stéphane had had to make do with second best. He tried to learn by watching. He tracked his father, just as his father tracked the game. He observed him for hours on end, noting every trick with the knife and rod, keeping himself out of sight, enjoying the thrill of seeing and not being seen, while at the same time half longing to be noticed.

The disadvantage of these holidays was loneliness. Even though he'd never got on well with Jean-Pierre, he missed him now. Jean-Pierre could be all right sometimes. Jean-Pierre had shown him how to do quite a few things, like lighting fires, and blacking your face if you didn't want to be seen moving around at night. But Jean-Pierre was in juvenile custody and not due to be released for months yet.

This morning, however, Stéphane had had no time to feel lonely. The first interesting thing had been the discovery of the mess round the hidy-hole in the wood. He'd gone to look at his stuff before anyone else was awake, while he was still in his pyjamas. Some animal, a big one by the look of it, had chewed up his matches and paper and rolled the torch deep into the burrow.

It must have been bigger than a rabbit or a squirrel. It must have been a fox, or a badger, or even a boar. He'd set off at once, and gone quite a long way up the lane, as far as the cave, but he hadn't seen anything.

He wasn't surprised. Wild things never showed themselves easily, he knew that much. He had the rest of the holidays in which to watch out for it, whatever it was.

He might even plan his own bit of poaching. He would give a lot to see his Dad's face when he came back with a catch of his own. He wasn't bothered by the loss of the matches. He had only taken them on the off chance that he might want to make a little fire somewhere, like he'd often done with Jean-Pierre last time they'd been here. It would be dead easy to take more. Mum had a whole packet of matchboxes. She would never miss one.

The next interesting, though rather alarming, event was the furious eruption of the farmer into the camp site just as Dad was sitting down to his breakfast. There was a loud hammering on the trailer door, and the enraged face of Monsieur Favier appeared, his scar showing up white in his scarlet face. He accused Dad of laying traps for trout in the stream, up by the ford. Dad was mystified at first, then self-righteously indignant.

"You're accusing me of setting traps in your dirty little stream?"

"Yes."

"I'm not taking that from you. I've never laid a fish trap in my life, and you've got no right to accuse me. I'll have you for defamation of character if you don't watch out. People don't mess with me and get away with it."

Monsieur Favier was obviously not convinced, but in fact, Monsieur Bourlaud was speaking the truth. He had never stooped to making fish traps. He did his poaching like a gentleman, with a rod and line.

There was a mystery here. Stéphane savoured it, probed at it, rolled it over in his mind.

Still in his pyjamas, he slipped out of the trailer when Monsieur Favier had had his say, and watched him climb back onto the tractor. A woman was perched on it too. She looked uncomfortable, as if she hardly ever hitched a ride on a tractor, as if she felt embarrassed being seen on it, with her legs dangling over the side, and her skirt riding up over her knees.

"I didn't know you were going to stop off here," she said to her husband. "I thought we were going straight down to search the cave."

He was still too angry to answer her. "Thieving scum," he said, starting up the engine. "They'd lie their way out of anything. Why do they have to choose *my* trout, in *my* stream, that's what I want to know? Why can't they take themselves off to the seaside for their holidays, like everyone else in Moulins?"

The tractor chugged off down the lane.

"Thieving scum!" mouthed Stéphane cheekily, mocking the angry farmer's departing back. "You'll never catch my Dad. He's too clever for you!"

The tractor disappeared round the corner. Stéphane suddenly remembered what the woman had said.

Going to search the cave, he thought. Now why would they be going to do that?

He knew the cave of course. He'd visited it several

times this year already, but with no one to talk to there, and nothing to do, he'd soon become bored.

He slid back into the trailer, moving deftly and economically as he always did when he wanted to remain unnoticed. He wriggled into his clothes, pushed his feet into his trainers, and silently edged outside again. His mother was cradling a cup of coffee in her hands and gazing vacantly out of the window. She didn't seem to see him.

His father, fiddling with the knobs on his radio, trying to find a sports programme, ignored him.

Stéphane set off in pursuit of the tractor.

He'd only covered half the distance to the cave when he heard the tractor coming back. He almost hid, then decided not to. He was anxious to learn more.

The farmer was still in a bad temper. He drew up alongside Stéphane, and raised his voice to make himself heard above the roar of the engine.

"Come here, you."

Stéphane took a reluctant step forward.

"Up to mischief I suppose, like that brother of yours?"

Stéphane said nothing. He'd learned to keep his mouth shut when he was being bawled out. For one thing, the shouting was usually over more quickly if he didn't join in. For another, he ran less risk of being hit. He'd also discovered that the less he said, the more the grown-ups talked. When they were angry they would say all kinds of things, pass on all sorts of information. Useful titbits. Secrets.

There was, at least, no risk of being hit by the farmer. If he showed any inclination to jump off his tractor, Stéphane would be away over the nearest field like a hunted hare.

"It couldn't possibly have been you, I suppose, who put that trap in my stream?" Monsieur Favier was saying, with heavy sarcasm.

Stéphane looked up at him impassively.

"And you didn't light a fire in my cave either?"

Stéphane stored away this interesting item, and waited.

Madame Favier touched her husband's arm. "It couldn't have been him, dear. He looks much too young. You said that trap was quite well made. Look at him. He can't be more than nine or ten."

Monsieur Favier grunted, unwilling to let Stéphane go. The memory of his burning barn,which he knew in his bones, had been the work of someone in this degenerate family, still gnawed at him.

Madame Favier leaned forward. "You haven't seen a boy around here, have you?"

Stéphane's sensitive ears picked up the kindness and anxiety in her voice. She's a soft touch, he thought. He shook his head, his eyes wide with inquiry.

"If you do see anyone, come and tell us," said Madame Favier. "Come up to the farm. I'll give you a nice piece of cake. He's an English boy. Must be about your age."

Stéphane nodded, hoping she would say more.

"You're wasting your time, Suzanne," said Monsieur Favier, putting his hand on his wife's knee and speaking much more gently. "I'm sure he's not anywhere round here. There was no sign of him last night, or this morning when I was down this way. And those ashes in the cave might have been there for months. They looked old to me, scattered and trampled all over the place like that."

"But what about the trap, Roland? It could easily have been him. The poor child must be starving by now. He's probably . . ."

"He's a city kid. Maurice said so. He'd never have the sense to make anything like that. I'm absolutely certain he's not on my land. I'd have found some trace of him by now, I know I would."

Madame Favier's soft mouth closed in an obstinate line, making her pouched cheeks pucker.

"Well, I don't agree, Roland. I've got a sort of feeling *here* . . ." She patted her stomach. "I won't feel happy till he's found."

Monsieur Favier sighed, let in the clutch and drove off. He had been looking forward to a peaceful Sunday. It was clearly going to be anything but that.

Stéphane watched the tractor until it was out of sight. A missing boy, from a city, who lit fires and trapped fish! The thought excited him and filled him with admiration. He'd often thought of going missing himself, running away and trying to manage on his own. He had never quite dared.

He decided at once to try and find the boy and see what he was like. He sounded as if he liked doing the things Stéphane wanted to do. He might be lonely, too.

He went cautiously along the lane towards the cave, walking silently on the grassy verge, and keeping his head below the level of the hedge so that no one would see him from the hillside above.

{25}

Peter stood on the hillside for a long time, not knowing whether to laugh or cry.

"No more rabbits," he told himself fiercely. "Whatever happens, no rabbits."

The words became a kind of chant in his head. "No rabbits. No rabbits. No rabbits."

The meaning began to dissolve as the rhythm of the words took over. They thumped away like the beat of a song. The sound felt triumphant at first, but then became depressing. Peter began to feel sad. He tried to shake the chant out of his head, so that he could think clearly. His fish trap had gone and he didn't dare make another. Rabbits were out of the question. That meant he'd have nothing but blackberries, unripe nuts and boiled leaves to eat today.

Yesterday he would have thought of giving up. He would have gone to the farm or the camp site. He would have overcome his fear of strangers and asked for help. The idea didn't even occur to him now. He felt wild and alone, hunted like the rabbit, sure that every man's hand would be turned against him.

He had to eat. That was the thought that obsessed him. That was the only idea in his head. Everything else had faded away.

Still standing in the shade of the old tree, he scanned the valley. Why couldn't humans eat grass, like those fat, contented cows? Why couldn't they peck grubs and insects out of the ground like that thrush?

People did eat insects sometimes, of course. Uncle Cliff had given Mum some bees coated in chocolate one Christmas, just to tease her. He knew how squeamish she was. Peter had tried one. It was crunchy, and all you tasted was the chocolate. No one had eaten the rest. They had gone mouldy, and been thrown away. He couldn't see himself eating bees again.

In his survival book there was a section about earthworms. You had to squeeze out the muck inside, and you could eat them raw or cook them in boiling water. He tried to imagine it, but his stomach rose in protest. He was hungry, but not that hungry. He would have to be starving before he sat down to eat a mass of worms.

The cows in the field below caught his attention. If only he'd learned to milk! He could have filled up his can and had a good filling drink, or even squirted the warm, creamy milk straight into his mouth from the cow's udder.

He looked up at the roof of the farm again, standing out above the trees. Presumably, the cows were taken up there to be milked. They would have been done this morning, before Scarface had brought them down to the field. The milk was probably still up at the farm, in a churn or something. If he was really careful, if he circled round and crept up on the cowshed from behind, he might be able to help himself to some.

The idea frightened him. There were plenty of people at school, hard kids like Scott and Colin, who took stuff from shops all the time. They had all the most expensive computer games and mobiles and watches, and they boasted of nicking really big things, DVDs, and bikes and TVs.

Peter had never stolen anything in his life. It wasn't so much that it was wrong. It was more that he hated the idea of being caught. Even taking a drink of milk from somebody else's churn made him shiver. He couldn't bear the idea of footsteps coming up behind him, and a heavy hand clamping down on his shoulder, and an angry voice accusing him.

I might not actually take anything, he thought. I'll just go up there and look round.

Something else as well as hunger was pushing him on. He wanted to look at a house, and be near people, even if he couldn't speak to them.

From his vantage point on the hillside he could see that the woods in front of the farm were thickest over to his left. He could get into them near the stream a quarter-of-a-mile or so along the lane, in the other direction from the camp site. That way he could approach the farm under cover, with no risk of being seen.

He thought for a moment of going back to the cave to get his can, but realized it would be quicker to cut across the hillside he was on, above the cave, and go to the farm direct.

There'll be ladles and things there that I could drink out of, he thought vaguely. He had no clear picture of a milking shed in his head. He'd never been in one.

It was further to the farm than he'd thought, and progress through the woods was difficult. A scrubby undergrowth of blackthorn and brambles kept blocking his way, and by the time he was at the top he was scratched all over the arms and legs, and very thirsty.

He came out of the wood behind the blank rear wall of a tall, windowless farm building, some kind of barn or shed. No one could have come round this side for years. Nettles grew chest high, and pieces of rusting machinery had all but disappeared under a mass of creepers and weeds. He couldn't even think of fighting his way through it.

He went back into the wood and cut across to the barbed wire fence a few metres further on. That was much more promising. He could see the back of the farmhouse now. It wasn't tidy and symmetrical like the front. There were no windows, only a collection of lean-tos and outhouses tacked onto the rough plaster wall. The door of one of these sheds was open, and a flock of white hens was pecking around in the beaten dusty earth of the doorway, strutting in and out with their bobbing, stilted gait. Inside, Peter could see tufts of straw and an old wooden frame studded with droppings.

"A hen-house," he breathed. "Eggs."

The sun was nearly overhead now and was beating down on the dry ground, bleaching the warm red from the old tiles on the roofs, and draining everything of its colour. There was no shade, no cover to be had at all between the edge of the wood and the hen-house. If Peter wanted eggs he would have to make a dash for the open door, and risk being caught out in the open. The hens would probably start squawking and flapping, and Scarface or someone would come running. He stood irresolute, not knowing what to do.

Then, a little further on beyond the house, near an old stone wall, he saw something else. It was a small cage on top of a post, like a bird table, roofed over with corrugated iron and walled in with wire netting. Inside it were three shelves and on them were small, white round things, set in saucers.

Goat's cheeses! Peter had seen cheeses set like that to dry in the Dordogne. He hadn't much liked their strong, farmyard flavour, but now his mouth was watering uncontrollably. The cheeses were food, satisfying, tasty, ready to simply pick up and eat. He had to restrain himself from scrambling under the barbed wire and running straight over to the cheese cage on a smash-and-grab raid.

Still behind the fence inside the wood, he inched through the prickly undergrowth in the direction of the cheese. Then he saw something else and grunted with satisfaction. There was a gap in the stone wall behind the cage. It gave a view of a well-stocked vegetable garden. Lettuces, leeks and cabbages grew in neat rows. There were taller, bushier plants as well, with long, finger-like things dangling from them.

Beans, I suppose, thought Peter.

Even better, a mass of bushy plants was bowing to the ground under trusses of huge ripe tomatoes.

Peter was under the barbed wire and stealing towards the gap in the wall before he'd realized what he was doing. He could already taste the sharp juiciness of a ripe tomato, and the creamy, salt tang of the cheese. He was almost dribbling.

Then behind him there was a rattling sound, and the growling whining voice of a dog building itself up to break into a ferocious outburst of barking. Before it found its full voice, the hens scattered in a shrieking cacophany that cut into the midday silence of the farmyard with the impact of a burst of machine gun fire.

Peter stood still, frozen to the ground. Then the dog, a young yellow mongrel with lips curled back over its teeth, rushed at him. Its chain brought it up short in mid-leap, as it went for a bite at Peter's arm.

Peter found that he was shaking, and his knees were weak, but he turned and ran to the nearest cover, the wall of the vegetable garden. He dived through the gap and threw himself down behind a row of runner beans, waiting for the pounding of footsteps to come after him.

Instead, he heard the sound of a car engine. It was coming towards the farmhouse from somewhere behind him. He was hidden by the stone wall, and with extreme caution he crawled back to the gap, and looked through it. What he saw was the last thing he'd expected, a man in uniform at the wheel of a dark blue car, which had a blue lamp on the roof. It was a gendarme in a police car.

He wanted to jump up, leap over the barbed wire and get back into the wood and away, down to the cave, the only place where he felt safe, but he couldn't move. His legs and arms, still trembling from the shock of being chased by the dog, felt like lead.

The car drove round to the front of the farmhouse out of sight, and stopped. The engine was switched off and Peter heard the car door open and shut, then feet scrunching on the gravel of the courtyard.

"Monsieur Favier! Vous êtes là? C'est moi, Daniel Chassot!"

There was silence, Peter could imagine the policeman standing at the front door of the farmhouse, knocking and waiting for someone to answer.

"Madame Favier, vous êtes là?"

His voice sounded relaxed, friendly even. A little of the rigidity went out of Peter's tensed up muscles. Perhaps he could, after all, go up to the gendarme and say . . . Say what? What would people think of him, skulking in a vegetable garden? They would know at once that he had come to steal. They would know already that he'd poached from Scarface's stream.

The gendarme's heavy shoes were on the gravel again. He was coming round to the back of the house, towards the wall behind which Peter was hiding. The dog was barking hysterically, rattling its chain noisily.

"Tais-toi, Katie. Qu-est-ce tu as?"

The dog's barking changed to an excited whiffling, snuffling noise. Peter could hear the man laugh, and the dog scuffling in the dust as it tried to jump up and lick him, and the man held its dirty paws away from his blue uniform trousers.

Then the gendarme's footsteps retreated again, round to the front of the farm. Peter heard the dog follow, yapping and whining as it asked for attention and another game.

"Monsieur Favier! Madame Favier! Y a personne?" the gendarme called again. He waited for a moment, then a door slammed, the engine started up and Peter dared look round the wall, to watch the car disappear away down the hill.

Silence descended on the farm.

There's no one here, thought Peter. His confidence was growing, putting out delicate, swift-growing shoots like a spring plant.

He stood up. Nothing happened. Katie was still at the front of the house where the gendarme had left her. Peter took a step forward. Still nothing happened.

There's no one here! he thought again jubilantly. He darted over to the nearest tomato plant, pulled off the biggest, reddest one in the bunch and sank his teeth into it. Juice dribbled down his chin and onto his T-shirt. He wiped himself with the back of his hand. The taste was so wonderful that tears came to his eyes.

He finished the tomato, and was about to eat another when he heard a sound from far down in the valley. Another car was coming this way. Scarface was probably on his way home. He might be here at any moment. Peter would be caught red-handed with tomato juice all over his shirt. But he still had a few minutes grace. He would take as much as he could while he had the chance.

Quickly, he took his anorak off from where it was still hanging round his waist, and tied the sleeves together to make a rough and ready bag. He loaded into it three huge tomatoes and a lettuce, then, almost dropping the precious load in his haste, he ran to the cheese cage. There were twelve succulent little rounds, four to each shelf, on separate white china saucers. Surely one would not be missed?

He hesitated for an agonising moment. If he left the empty saucer the theft would be noticed at once. If he took the saucer he'd have to dispose of it carefully, or it would give him away.

The car was turning the corner below the farm. The dog's chain was rattling. Kate would be standing up again, all her senses alert. If she came round the corner of the house to meet the car, she'd see him again and all hell would break loose.

Quickly, he lifted a saucer from the middle shelf and placed it and its contents in his anorak. Then, with shaking fingers, he pushed back the catch of the cheese cage door, put both arms round his load to prevent anything falling out, and ran like a hare, low to the ground, back to the barbed wire fence that edged the wood.

He had only just scrambled under it and crashed through a thicket of hazels to the cover of the wood beyond when the car drew up outside the farmhouse. He heard the dog's rapturous barks of welcome, and a voice which somehow he knew to be Scarface's.

"Ça suffit, Katie! Arrêtes!"

Silently, Peter slipped through the wood and down the hill towards the cave. He wouldn't eat until he got there, then he would gorge himself on this wonderful food. Later, when it was dark, he would risk another visit. He would watch to see when the people were out, and come back for more vegetables and eggs. He would find out where the milk was kept, and look for other things.

He was a real outlaw now. A vagabond. A thief.

{26}

A huge red truck, headlights flashing, roared up alongside Mr Castle's car, its horn blaring. Mr Castle craned his neck upwards to see the driver in the cab above mouthing abuse and gesticulating obscenely. He yelled rudely in reply, then turned his attention back to the motorway. What had he done wrong? Why had the truck driver lost his cool?

The motorway stretched endlessly onward through mile after mile of central France, with its rolling prairie and thick forest. Mr Castle rubbed his tired eyes. Perhaps he had shut them for a second or two. Perhaps he had swerved out of his lane. He shivered, in spite of the heat. If he fell asleep at the wheel and crashed . . .

A sign at the side of the road indicated the turning to a service station. He took a sudden decision and pulled over to the right, cutting in front of a fast-moving petrol tanker, which had to brake sharply. Mr Castle felt beads of sweat break out on his scalp. It was definitely time for a rest.

He stopped the car in the car park and took out his mobile. Mrs Castle answered at once. Her hand must have been hovering over the phone, waiting for it to ring.

"Where are you, Tom? Have you found the turn-off?"

"Give me a chance, Rosemary. I haven't even got to

Moulins. I suppose they still want me to report to the gendarmerie there before I do anything else?"

"How should I know? The police here haven't deigned to ring me since last time you phoned. There hasn't been one single call from anyone."

He could hear a sob gathering in her voice and spoke quickly to forestall it.

"Listen, I'll call again from Moulins. I should be there in under an hour. They might have some information by then from the local people. You've got to relax. Do your yoga exercises or something. You don't want to be a wreck for Peter when . . ."

He could hear her trying to control her tears, not trusting herself to speak.

"I'll call you soon, in an hour or two. Love to Rachel. 'Bye."

Sitting on a hard chair in the gendarme headquarters in Moulins, Mr Castle felt his first glimmer of comfort since this whole terrible business had begun. There was an efficiency, a neatness, a sense of regimented control about this place. It was different from the more relaxed, civilian atmosphere of an English police station. He found it soothing.

He had been expected. Messages had gone humming down the wires from Dover to Maidstone, from Maidstone to Interpol in Lyons. Orders had cascaded down the gendarme military hierarchy, orders to search, orders to spread the news of the missing boy, orders to ask questions. For the first time he appreciated the care they'd taken in Dover, the details they'd asked for, so seemingly irrelevant at the time, so reassuringly complete now.

The gendarme major came to the door of his inner sanctum to receive him with a formal handshake. He had already spread out a large map on his table, and a sheaf of papers was neatly stacked beside it. The top one had a photograph of Peter, a black and white print-out of the colour snap Rosemary had snatched off the mantlepiece in the front room in the early hours of this morning. Mr Castle, dropping into the chair beside the major's desk, almost burst into tears at the sight of it.

The direct, unsmiling appraisal in the major's eyes stopped him. Mr Castle felt again the appalling weight of guilt that had been crushing him since that ghastly moment in Dover when he'd found that Peter was missing. What could this soldierly man be thinking of a father who'd carelessly left his son in a strange country, who hardly even knew where to start looking?

"This has been the worst day of my life," he said at last, half to himself, not knowing whether or not the major could speak English.

The major seemed to understand. He nodded, and went on looking at him, saying nothing. A dreadful idea occurred to Mr Castle.

It's as if he thinks . . . He might suspect . . .

He couldn't bear to frame the thought in words. He'd read of cases in the paper where parents who'd murdered their children had reported them missing to put the police off the scent. Was that what they thought of him? That he'd murdered Peter, and was trying to cover it up? Was that why the policeman in Dover had tried to make him stay at home, where they could easily pick him up when they found . . .

He tried to pull himself together. They would discover soon enough that nothing awful had happened. Peter was lost, that was all. He would be found very soon now. That was the only thing that mattered – to find him. He looked down at the map.

"It was near a cave and a stream," he said lamely. "We stopped for a picnic."

Again the major nodded. He picked up a paper from the pile.

"I have here a list of all the possible places in the area," he said slowly in French. Mr Castle was relieved to find he could understand. His French was patchy, to say the least, but they would get by, he hoped, if both spoke slowly in their own language. Like him, the major clearly found it easier to understand a foreign language than to speak it.

The caves had been lightly circled on the map in pencil. Eagerly, Mr Castle pored over it. If only he'd noticed more about the place! If only he'd looked at the names of the villages! He'd been too busy admiring the scenery in a general kind of way, looking out for a nice place to picnic, and revelling in Billie's relaxed, amusing company, so different from . . . He'd been a total fool.

The major broke in on his thoughts. "After you left the autoroute, did you pass through any villages?"

"Yes – no – I think so. Yes, I'm sure we did. We went a long way off the road. We felt we had plenty of time. We wanted to have a good long break, enjoy the countryside . . ."

"Did you notice any particular buildings, a church perhaps, or a château?"

Mr Castle shut his eyes, desperately trying to think. There had been a château. Billie had pointed it out. "I wouldn't mind living there," she'd said. "It's time I found a rich man to keep me in style." He tried not to remember the silly thing he'd said in reply. He tried to focus on the château.

"It was on a hill-top, surrounded by woods." His eyes were screwed up tight shut, as he desperately tried to visualize it. "It was a mile or so before we got to the cave, I think. It had a round tower. Maybe two."

The major called through the half-open door of his office.

"Pagny! You're a local man. Does this mean anything to you? Château on a hill, woods all round, one, possibly two round towers?"

The young gendarme slowly shook his head.

"Could be a number of places. Do you want me to circulate it?"

"Not yet. Now, Monsieur Castle, did you pass any churches? Cross any bridges? See a railway line?"

"I just don't remember," said Mr Castle helplessly.

"There might have been a church. Grey stone."

"Every church in the *département* is built of grey stone. There must be thousands of them." A slight tartness had entered the major's voice. "Now, let's return to the autoroute. Had you passed the turn-off to Moulins?"

"Possibly. I think so. I mean, we might have."

The major's finger had been hovering over a circle surrounding the words 'St Didier-des-Bois.' He moved it slowly up the map, and it came to a halt over a cluster of circles in the curve of a long blue line.

"In my judgement we should concentrate our preliminary search here." He stabbed at the map with a decisive forefinger. "We will continue of course to mobilise the whole *département*, but we will ask you, Monsieur Castle, to accompany our men first to this point."

Mr Castle stared dumbly at the map, and nodded. The major stood up and came round from behind his desk. He put a hand on Mr Castle's shoulder. His military manner slipped for a moment, and his humanity shone through.

"Cheer up, my poor friend. We will find your Peter, safe and well, I'm sure of it. I have a son too. I understand how you feel."

Mr Castle shook his head despondently.

"How did I – how could I have . . .?"

"We are all human. We make mistakes. Do not reproach yourself."

His tone became suddenly brisk again.

"When did you last eat?"

"Eat? I don't know. I suppose – yesterday, the picnic, where . . . I'm not hungry. I couldn't eat a thing."

"But this is absurd. You must keep up your strength. You have a long day ahead, maybe even another night. Pagny! Bring a snack for Monsieur Castle. A glass of wine, a sandwich, some coffee. Now, Monsieur Castle, a few more details before you set off. I hope you have brought with you a garment belonging to Peter?"

"A garment? Yes, I think so. There's a sweater of his in the car. Why?"

"It may be necessary, if, for example, there is a need to use dogs in the search."

"Dogs? Oh, but surely, that would mean . . ."

"Please, Monsieur Castle, do not distress yourself. We are professionals. We have to be prepared for all eventualities."

{27}

Stéphane had made a minute examination of the cave. He'd noticed everything. He'd seen the prints of Peter's trainers and reckoned by their size that they must belong to the boy. He'd seen the two tins and the plastic bottle in the crevice, and had correctly interpreted the black soot stains on the larger tin.

He's been cooking in here, he thought, pleased with his powers of deduction. Trust that stupid farmer not to work that out.

Near the wood pile, that at first glance he had taken for debris from the green funnel at the back of the cave, he stopped and sniffed. He squatted down and ferreted about in the twigs until he found two spiny skeletons and the remains of a pair of fish heads. Then he sat back on his heels and thought.

The fish trap in the river – that must have been the boy's. He nodded with appreciation. It must have been good if the boy had caught these two big fish in it. He wished he'd seen it. And then there were the matches. He'd already found the matchbox with the half match still in it, tucked into the cubby hole in the rock wall. The boy had taken them and covered his tracks to make him think an animal had rooted them up. He must be clever. He'd be a friend worth having.

The boy must be out somewhere now, hunting or trapping. He'd be up in the woods probably, after rabbits or pheasants. Stéphane frowned, thinking hard. If the boy was setting traps, poaching stuff, and if he wasn't found, it would be Dad who would get the blame. Dad might even get arrested and taken off. He'd done time for petty theft before. They would be sure to do him properly for poaching.

Stéphane tapped his knees reflectively with his fingers. He did, in fact, remember the months that Monsieur Bourlaud had spent in prison as the happiest of his entire life. It wasn't only that he had guiltily enjoyed the absence of his father. The really wonderful thing had been the transformation of his mother.

Madame Bourlaud had seemed to grow miraculously young again. She'd stopped nagging him about coming in late and getting his clothes dirty, and had taken to chatting with him, as if he was an adult. She'd even collapsed into uncontrollable giggles one happy evening, when they'd sat up late together and watched an old comedy on TV. One day, he noticed that she was looking almost pretty, and he'd felt proud of her for the first time in his life.

He remembered, too, that there had been a bit of money in the house. His mother had had the family allowance for herself. She'd spent some of it on him, on some new shoes, and the jacket he'd wanted for months and months.

Dad had put a stop to all that, of course, as soon as he

was home. The money went straight into his pocket and straight out again, into the till of the Boule d'Or, the café on the corner. Stéphane hadn't minded that so much as the gloom that had returned to the house with his father's home-coming. The nagging, the dreariness and a constant underlying fear had come in through the front door with him.

He'd been squatting for too long and he was getting pins and needles in his legs. He stood up, and his mind turned back to the boy. What was he doing here, all alone, an English boy in France?

He's bunked off, thought Stéphane admiringly. His Dad beat him up. He's had enough and he's bunked off.

The idea pleased him. He was going to do that, as soon as he could. He was going to run away and live somewhere, out of reach of his Dad's fists.

I'll give him a bit of help, he thought. He'll need things like matches, and food, and stuff like that.

He stood up and pulled out of his pocket the full match box he had taken from the trailer that morning. He took half the matches out, and stuffed them into Peter's box, then put it back where he'd found it, in its hiding place.

Outside, a blackbird's startled alarm call made him jump. He looked round quickly. The boy would be angry if he caught him in the cave. He might suspect him of something. Everything would start off wrong. Anyway, it was too soon to actually meet him face to face. Stéphane would prefer to see him first, to check him out until he felt he knew him. He'd watch him from a safe distance, like he watched his father.

The blackbird squawked again, from near the entrance to the cave. It was too late to get out that way. He would have to scramble up the narrow opening at the back of the cave.

Moving almost as fast as the two lizards, who had whisked themselves out of sight as soon as he'd passed their rock, Stéphane scrambled over Peter's fuel pile, and fought his way up the funnel, clutching at tufts of grass that came away in his hands, and knocking down clods of earth with his feet, his sheer momentum pushing him on.

With a last heave he made it to the top, and wriggled his small body through the long grass and thistles that fringed the funnel's edge. As soon as he was sure he was out of sight from the cave below, he flopped down panting, listening as hard as he could, even picking up the faint distant sound of the cows' long teeth tearing at the grass in the field below, in spite of the loud hammering of his pulse in his ears.

There was no other sound at all. No footsteps in the lane, no crunching of leaves underfoot in the wood, nothing at all that signalled the presence of another human being. He waited for a long time, then cautiously moved to a more comfortable position. That stupid blackbird must have seen a fox or something. It had given a false alarm.

The sun was almost overhead now, and the air was still very hot.

It's not bad here, thought Stéphane. He was lying on

a patch of silky grass with a scrubby growth of young trees overhead which made a pleasant shade. He wriggled forward a couple of metres and looked down the funnel into the cave. The sun was striking directly into it, illuminating the whole back half. If he kept still, and made sure that the fanned out spikes of a clump of grass covered his face, he'd be able to peer through them and watch the boy quite well. Even if the boy looked up, he'd be blinded by the sun and wouldn't recognise the round dark blob overhead as a human head. Stéphane was glad he'd found this place. It was a good place. It felt lucky.

He lay still, idly watching a bee as it fumbled round a spike of yellow flowers.

"You get near me and I'll gut you," he muttered. Then his eyes began to close.

Sounds in the cave below woke him. He opened his eyes and lay still for a moment, trying to work out where he was. Then he remembered, and his heart started thumping. The boy must be back! Slowly, with infinite care, he lifted his head and looked down the funnel. He could clearly hear someone moving about. He could hear shoes slipping on the stones. But the light was disappointing. The sun had moved some distance since he had shut his eyes, and it now lit up only the pile of sticks, and a few square feet of the cave's rocky floor beyond it. The rest was in deep shadow.

Then, in the shadow, he saw something move and cautiously lowered his head behind the clump of grass.

He could make out no more than a pale shape, the outline of a white T-shirt and the top of a head covered with light brown hair.

There was a flash of something shiny, and a sploshing, gulping sound. The boy was drinking from a plastic bottle, holding it above his head and draining it. For a moment, Stéphane saw his face. It was quite thin and very dirty, but even in that brief instant he could see that it was an open kind of face, the sort that might be friendly. The boy looked a bit like Michel Leclos, the quiet one, the one he liked best in his class at school. He had none of the tightness, the meanness, of Paul Durand, Stéphane's chief tormentor, and the pack of playground rats he led.

The boy put the empty bottle down and moved just out of sight towards the front of the cave. The sun glittered on something he'd put down on the rock beside the bottle. Stéphane craned his neck to see what it was, and drew in his breath.

The boy had a Swiss army knife, a wonderful penknife, dark red with the Swiss cross engraved on its side. It was a fat one. It must have all the blades. It was the thing Stéphane had longed for more than anything else in his whole life. He had spent hours during the past year, gazing through the window of the hunting shop in Moulins, practically licking the glass, drinking in the glory of the knife on show, which spun slowly round on its little electric turntable, showing off its cutting blades, its saw, its scissors, its bottle opener, and its screwdriver.

He wanted desperately to hold the boy's knife and try it out himself. If he was careful, and approached the boy in the right way, showed he was friendly and wanted to help him the boy might let him have a go with it. He might want to be friends. It wasn't very likely. He didn't get on with anyone at school, so there was no reason to think that a stranger, who wasn't even French, would treat him any differently, but it was a good thought. He would be even more careful to take things slowly, and make the boy grateful before he risked showing himself.

A brown hand, scratched and stained, suddenly shot out of the shadows, picked up the knife and disappeared. Stéphane listened. The boy seemed to be eating. He was making slurping noises, as if he was biting into something juicy. Stéphane delicately wrinkled his nose and picked up the faint tang of a ripe tomato.

He must have been at the farm, he thought, remembering Madame Favier's vegetable garden. They won't like that. They might do Dad for that.

The noise and smell of eating reminded him that he was starving himself. They would be eating soon, his Mum and Dad, and if he was late there would be angry words and the risk of getting no lunch at all.

Silent as a fox, he slid backwards through the grass, went round in a long loop through the wood and over the hillside, and slipped into his chair by the table Mum had set up outside the trailer just before Monsieur Bourlaud sat himself heavily down in his.

"What've you been up to all morning? Hanging round

that farm, I suppose. Thought I told you to stay away from there?"

"I haven't been anywhere near it, Dad, honest. Just up the lane. Saw a hare running near the wood."

Monsieur Bourlaud took a swig of wine, pleased with the information. He would work out how to lift the hare after lunch, before his pleasant afternoon torpor turned to sleep.

{28}

By the time Peter had eaten his three large tomatoes, the whole lettuce and most of the goat's cheese he was no longer hungry. He wasn't really satisfied however. He wanted something solid and filling, like bread or potatoes.

He could feel the unaccustomed food he'd eaten during the last twenty-four hours, the masses of blackberries, the rich cheese, the unripe nuts, the half-cooked fish and last night's strange vegetables churning round in his gut. He felt windy and uncomfortable. Twice he had to bend double as cramp pains shot through his abdomen. They passed off quickly, but they frightened him.

I might get ill, he thought, and the image of himself lying sick and abandoned in the cave made his eyelids prickle with tears of self-pity.

He finished the cheese slowly, nibbling round the edges and swallowing it crumb by crumb. He was getting used to the goaty taste – quite liking it, in fact – but the saltiness made him thirsty. He looked regretfully at the empty plastic bottle, wishing he hadn't finished the water off before he'd started to eat. Now he would have to go down to the spring again.

He wasn't sure why, but he was glad to be out of the

cave, even though the sun was almost unbearably hot out in the open. He'd felt uneasy in there since he'd come back with his loot from the farm. Everything had looked the same. Robert and Stripey had been out on their rock, peacefully sunning themselves, his things were still in the crevice and there was no sound from outside, except for the occasional movement of the cows in the field nearby, and the mewing of the buzzard high up in the sky over the woods. But still he felt nervy and watchful, less safe than he'd felt before.

It took him a while to get to the spring. He had to skirt round the edge of the field now that it was full of cows. He wasn't afraid of walking through them, he told himself. He just thought it would be silly to set them off mooing and running about, attracting attention from anyone who might be in the woods or coming up the lane.

Then, too, he needed to keep his eyes open. He needed to search every inch of hedge and every clump of trees he passed in case there was a source of food he'd missed before. He was rewarded by a find of fresh young chickweed and a handful of green hazelnuts.

He filled his bottle at the spring, and took a good long drink from it. The cool, delicious water seemed to settle the growling of his stomach and lifted his spirits.

He picked his way over the stones that stuck out of the mud at the foot of the spring and began to wander back along the bank of the stream. It was nice here, cool and refreshing. The clouds of gnats that had tangled in his hair last night had disappeared. The rippling of the water through the stones was soothing.

He found a good place, where a low bank of soft grass fringed a patch of smooth dry sand, and sat down, leaning his back against the grass. It was comfortable, almost like sitting in an armchair. He wriggled his bottom into the sand to make a soft hollow, and stretched out his legs.

A gigantic yawn convulsed him. He was exhausted all of a sudden. He'd intended to go back to the cave and get to work on making a handle for his soup can, get a good pile of firewood together and find food for supper, but the thought of leaving the shade of the trees again for the broiling sun outside was too much. He'd stay here where it was cool for a while and rest. His disturbed night was catching up with him.

He dozed off and on for an hour or more, and woke with a sob in his throat. An upsetting dream was drifting out of his mind. He could only catch hold of its insubstantial tail. He had felt alone and threatened. Something safe and familiar, something to do with home, had turned on him and let him down. He couldn't quite remember what it had been about.

His arm itched. He started scratching and looked down to see a series of four or five bites running up the soft inside part of his arm. The tell-tale whine of a mosquito droned round his head. He slapped irritably at it, and missed.

He got to his feet, feeling woozy and depressed. He

wasn't hungry again quite yet, but he soon would be. The thought didn't worry him much any more. He could deal with hunger. He'd foraged successfully for the past twenty-four hours and could do it again, he felt sure. The real problem was loneliness. It was pecking away at his mind like a famished crow, and soon it would be tearing and devouring. He'd have to conquer it somehow, if he was going to hold out here for the rest of the day, and for another night, and maybe tomorrow, and tomorrow night, and . . .

I can't stay here forever, he thought, beginning to run through the field, oblivious now of the cows and the attention they might attract as they sheered nervously away in front of him. The weather'll change, and it'll get cold, and I haven't got any warm clothes.

A picture came into his mind. He saw the autoroute running northwards from the Dordogne to Calais. It rolled across the vastness of France, over hills, through plains, skirting cities, until at last it stopped at the sea. An endless wave of cars, trucks and coaches rolled along it. If he could only find his way back to it, to the place where they had turned off for the picnic (which seemed at least a year ago), he could surely be carried north along with it, thumb a lift, or hide in the back of a van. Then at Calais he could stow away in a truck or the boot of a car, and once in England he'd go to the police. It would be safe to do that there. The English police would hardly be interested in a bit of poaching in France. He'd make them take him home without telephoning first, and he'd just walk in through the door, and watch their faces, and . . .

The dream he'd forgotten suddenly came back to him, and slowed him down to a dragging walking pace. He'd gone home in his dream, only Mum hadn't been there. Billie had opened the door. She was wearing Mum's best dress and had had her hair done like Mum's. Julian was standing beside her with Peter's brand new football tucked under his arm.

"Oh, it's you," Billie had said. "You don't live here any more, I'm afraid," and she had shut the door.

"Bitch," muttered Peter, tightening his fingers. He felt the plastic bottle creak in his hands and hurriedly loosened them. He couldn't afford to split it, and lose his only water container.

He was back at the cave already. He put the bottle down carefully in its old place. At least the cave felt good again. The edgy feeling had gone. It was as cool here as it had been by the stream, and there were no mosquitos.

I wish the rock wasn't so hard to lie on though, thought Peter. He remembered the softness of the sand by the stream, and the cushion-like comfort of the grassy bank behind his back. He would have to make something like that in the cave, something like a bed or a pillow.

He went outside and collected a big pile of dry grass, brought it back inside, patted it into shape and tried lying down on it. It squashed down at once, and he could feel the hard edges of the uneven floor through it, but it was still good, far better than the bare rock had been, and less scratchy than he'd expected.

I'll get an extra lot for a pillow, he thought, and cover it with dry moss, and then I can keep my anorak over me in the night.

He spent a long time making his bed, and arranging the moss properly. He'd cheered up again. He almost began to look forward to the darkness, when he could lie down comfortably and watch the flames of a friendly fire. He was sure now he'd be able to light it with his one short split match. He was sure he wouldn't be afraid.

But first he'd have to collect firewood, and find some things for his evening soup, and make a handle for his can. He had a lot of work to do in what remained of the afternoon.

He toyed with the idea of making another fish trap further down the stream, where the farmer would be less likely to find it, but decided against it. He'd had enough of the stream for the time being. It no longer seemed cool and inviting, but treacherous and sinister. In any case, he didn't want any more bites. The ones he had were itchy enough already.

He had another idea. Up near the farm he had seen a field of yellow wheat stubble. He knew it was wheat because he'd noticed some loose ears, lying at the edge of the field. He'd often eaten raw wheat on country walks. He'd snapped off a few plump ears, rubbed them between the palms of his hands to loosen the chaff and picked out the delicious milky grains. If he managed to find a good few, he could cook them in his soup along with the chickweed he'd found earlier. It would be more filling, more like real food.

While he was up there, he might take a look at the vegetable garden again. He wouldn't plan anything. He'd just see if anyone was around, if the dog was round at the front of the house, or if the hens had strayed away from the door of the hen-house.

It was still only the middle of the afternoon, though the day seemed to have been going on forever. He would make the can-handle first, and think out a better method of balancing it on the fire.

He'd look for more wire later, on his way up to the wheat field. He'd need it for tomorrow and the next day, when he got around to making more and better gadgets, grills for cooking, and traps. He wouldn't make a fool of himself again, like he had this morning, with the rabbit. He would try trapping a bird, a pheasant or a pigeon. He was sure it would be quite different, much easier, than killing a rabbit.

{29}

Monsieur Gérard took another sip from the glass of cognac which his old friend had just filled, pushed his chair back from the table, stretched out his legs and folded his plump hands over his well-rounded stomach. He was full of Sunday afternoon contentment.

"Wonderful cook, your wife," he said, letting out a satisfied yawn. "That roast pork – tenderest I've ever tasted."

Monsieur Favier acknowledged the compliment with a half smile. Since Maurice's wife had died, he had been looked after by a sharp nosed daughter whose mail order business left little time for good old-fashioned cooking. His regular invitation to join the Faviers for Sunday lunch was the high point of Maurice's week.

"And the apple tart . . ."

"Yes, yes, I know." Maurice would sing Suzanne's praises for ever, once he got started, but Monsieur Favier had other things on his mind. "Now look here, Maurice, are you seriously suggesting that I should donate – actually *donate* – one of my prize turkeys for this competition of yours? I don't even play bowls myself."

Monsieur Gérard smoothed the wings of grey hair on each side of his rosy bald crown, and sat up again, crossing his legs. A good wrangle with Roland was just what he needed to lever him out of the torpor that always overcame him after one of Suzanne's lunches. He felt in the breast pocket of his linen jacket, and pulled out a sheet of bright yellow paper, which he unfolded and spread out on the tablecloth. It made a bold splash against the blue checks and pink roses that rioted over the plastic cloth.

Monsieur Gérard fished his reading glasses out of another hidden recess and perched them on his nose with the measured deliberation which had impressed generations of school children.

"*Councours de Pétanques,*" he read out. "Sunday 28th August. First prize, a grade-one turkey."

"All right, all right," said Monsieur Favier impatiently. "I can read, you know. But it's all a trick. I never actually promised . . ."

He picked the notice up, and held it towards the faint light that penetrated the cool, dimly-lit room through the crocheted curtains. He smiled in spite of himself as he read down the list of competing villages.

"Dompierre? Vitry? However did you get them involved? They've been at each other's throats for years. You'll have a pitched battle on your hands instead of a game of bowls if you're not careful."

Monsieur Gérard tilted his head back and looked down his nose.

"We mayors have the best interests of our *communes* at heart," he began pompously. "That kind of damaging juvenile rivalry is a thing of the past. Anyway . . ."

Monsieur Favier snorted.

"Anyway, you want one of my turkeys. And for nothing. What do you think I am – made of money? Do you know how much I was offered at last Thursday's cattle market for two of my calves? Go on, guess!"

Monsieur Gérard took another sip of cognac. Once Roland started on the miseries of being a farmer it would take more than the prospect of an inter-village bowls competition to stop him. He listened and nodded sympathetically, in gratitude for his lunch. Then, through Monsieur Favier's embittered complaints, he became aware of another noise, the rattle of a chain and frenzied barking.

"What's the matter with that dog of yours?"

"Katie? Oh, I don't know. A fox or something, I expect. Suzanne'll see to it."

Monsieur Gérard looked automatically towards the armchair in the corner of the room in which Madame Favier usually spent her Sunday afternoons comfortably ensconced with her knitting, absorbed in the Sunday film on TV. For once the chair was empty.

"Suzanne all right?" he asked delicately.

Monsieur Favier grimaced.

"Restless," he said. "She's taken this business of the missing English boy to heart. Says she's sure he's round here somewhere. She made me go down and search the cave this morning. No sign, of course."

Monsieur Gérard said nothing. Madame Favier had never got over the loss of her only child, a boy, in the first week of his life. It had happened thirty years ago, but she was still subject to irrational fancies concerning children. Both men were used to them, and accepted them with a mystified tolerance.

The dog was still barking.

"It's round the back, by the hen house," said Monsieur Favier, getting unwillingly to his feet. "I'd better go and look."

He pushed through the plastic fronds hanging in the doorway that led directly from the living room of the farmhouse into the yard outside. Monsieur Gérard idly listened to his footsteps as he started round the corner of the house, then he heard him turn back. A car was bumping up the rough lane.

Monsieur Gérard went to the door himself. He was in time to see Daniel Chassot jump out of the blue police car.

"Monsieur Gérard! *Bonjour*. I hoped I would find you here."

Katie ran up, dragging her chain, and wagging her entire rear end in her pleasure at seeing the gendarme. He stepped back, out of reach of her dusty paws, but she didn't follow him. Instead, she bounded off again, back towards the vegetable garden, where she stood motionless, her ears cocked, watching and listening.

The three men took no notice of her.

"Well, Chassot?" said Monsieur Gérard, puffing out his cheeks and assuming the official manner which he had acquired during his many years of schoolteaching.

The gendarme unconsciously stood to attention.

"We've received some further information, sir, on the missing English boy. The father has arrived at Moulins, and has started his search further north. He's being taken to various likely sites to see if he can recognise the place where the boy was lost."

"You mean he doesn't even know where it was?" interrupted Monsieur Favier in disgust. "Must be a complete idiot."

"He's English," said Monsieur Gérard with a shrug. "This is a foreign country to him. I sympathize. I understand. If you had ever been to England, Roland . . ."

"Me? Go to England?" Monsieur Favier sounded indignant. "The food's uneatable and it never stops raining. And anyway, where would I find the time or the money? It's all very well for schoolteachers, on the salaries they earn. Before you retired on that inflated pension of yours, you used to spend more time on holiday than you did at work. Farmers . . ."

Daniel Chassot shuffled his feet. He knew these two of old. Once launched into an argument they'd be capable of going on all day unless they were forcibly interrupted. He tried to think of a tactful way of doing it. At that moment, fortunately, the computer terminal in his car bleeped, saving him the trouble. He opened the front passenger door, sat down, and lowered the lid in which the keyboard was set, then read the message coming through on the screen.

Monsieur Gérard and Monsieur Favier followed him

and bent to look into the car. They watched the message appear with fascinated respect.

Chassot tapped a few keys in a masterful manner.

"They've drawn a blank so far," he said. "They're working their way south."

"Clever machine you've got there," said Monsieur Favier. "How does it work?"

Monsieur Gérard straightened himself, anxious to reassert his authority.

"Never mind that now, Roland. Tell me, Chassot, when do they expect to get down here?"

"Difficult to say, sir. There are still a fair number of likely areas to follow up, and it's nearly five o'clock already. They're taking care not to overdo it, in case the father gets confused. They'll have to call a halt when the light goes. They may get here this evening, but it's more likely to be first thing tomorrow morning. If the father says this is the right area, and if the boy hasn't turned up, we'll have to bring in a dog, and do a field-to-field search."

Monsieur Gérard found to his annoyance that he was now standing to attention. He shifted his weight onto one foot, and crossed his arms.

"I see. How many men does the chief of your brigade want if there's to be a search?"

"As many as possible. Everyone we can muster. But it's not very likely to come to that. It'll only be necessary if the father says this is the right place."

A breathless, perspiring Madame Favier came running

round the corner of the house, her mules slapping on the hard baked ground.

"I saw him! I know I did! It was the English boy – I'm sure of it! Running down the hill he was, with a bundle in his arms. He'd been in the hen house. Look, he dropped these bits of wheat. Didn't you hear Katie barking? Poor child, I'd give him all my eggs. He must be so hungry, so frightened. I can't bear to think . . ."

Monsieur Favier took his wife's arm and gently shook it.

"Come on, Suzanne, it was probably the Bourlaud boy. Little thief – just like him to hang round here and help himself to your eggs."

Madame Favier shook her head.

"It was him, I'm sure it was!" she said, tears in her voice. "He ran in an English sort of way!"

Daniel Chassot hid a smile and cleared his throat.

"Can you describe the boy, Madame?"

She looked vaguely at him.

"Not really, I hardly saw him. He was a boy, quite small, with a pale sort of shirt."

"The Bourlaud brat was wearing a white shirt," growled Favier.

"Colour of hair? Colour of eyes?"

"I couldn't really say."

"Was he wearing a jacket? Shorts or trousers?"

"I didn't notice. I just saw him dart off over the wall and into the wood."

Monsieur Favier and Daniel Chassot exchanged

expressive looks.

"Thank you very much, Madame," said Chassot, closing the keyboard of his Saphir terminal."I'll have to be on my way now. I've got to get round the other *communes* and contact all the mayors."

"But aren't you going to follow him?" said Madame Favier looking distressed. "He went down that way, through the wood, towards the stream."

Chassot followed the direction of her finger. She was pointing straight towards the camp site.

"We'll follow it up in due course, Madame, when we've established that this is the correct area. Goodbye, Monsieur Favier. Monsieur le Maire, I'll call you later on as soon as I have more information."

He slammed the car door and drove away.

{30}

Stéphane had perfected a devious route from the camp site to the cave. It involved creeping along the ditch by the lane for a hundred metres or so, ducking through a hole in the hedge, skirting a field to get down to the stream, slipping from one willow to another as far as the next field boundary, and doubling back up to the cave in the lee of another hedge.

He had intended to go back to the cave straight after lunch, but there had been too much going on at the camp site. Another family had turned up, people from Nevers. They looked posh, a bit soft, saying "Oh darling" to each other, but they had a boy with them, Nicholas, a year or so younger than Stéphane, who might turn out all right, for a bit of football at least.

In any case, Stéphane hadn't wanted to set off without some stuff for the boy at the cave, some sweets and biscuits and things like that. He'd wanted to get a saucepan, too. That old tin can of the boy's looked useless for cooking anything, but Mum had sat in the trailer all afternoon, stuck in front of the Sunday film, and it had been impossible to get near the kitchen cupboard. In the end he'd had to make do with a couple of cellophane wrapped toffees, which had been in his jacket pocket for the last three weeks at least.

His elaborate efforts to approach the cave unseen were wasted. No one was there. He watched and listened for a long time before he dared go in. Then he looked round, impressed. The boy had been busy. The bed looked good, neatly made and quite comfortable. Stéphane badly wanted to lie on it, but was afraid of leaving too obvious traces of himself.

He noticed the new wire handle on the can, picked it up and examined it closely. It was clever. He was eager to see how it would work on the fire. He would like to be in here, squatting beside the boy, while he cooked his supper, helping him, cutting things up for him with the knife, talking to him. He would watch and wait for the right moment, and when it came he would show himself and say – say what?

A footstep outside set the hair on his scalp tingling. Quick as a flash he whipped the sweets out of his pocket, dropped them on the ground beside the can and made for the green funnel. He had only just hauled himself over the lip and dropped panting onto the silky grass above when he heard the boy's voice.

"Hi, Robert. What's happened to Stripey?"

Stéphane's nose twitched with puzzlement. What kind of rubbish was that he was speaking? It took him a moment to work it out.

English! Of course, the boy was speaking English! He probably couldn't speak French at all.

The dream of friendship that had flowered in Stéphane's mind lost its rosiness. For a moment he was angry.

He wanted to heave a rock down the funnel and hit the boy, hurt him and give him a fright he would never forget, but the anger passed quickly. Curiosity took its place.

So what if he and the boy couldn't speak to each other? It didn't have to matter that much. Most people never said anything worth listening to anyway. They could still be friends.

Stéphane had dropped the sweets directly below the funnel, where he could see them from above. As he watched, the top of the boy's head came into view. He hadn't noticed the sweets yet. He was putting a bundle down on the ground beside the fuel pile.

He opened the bundle, spreading it out, and Stéphane cautiously craned his neck, watchful in case his head cast a tell-tale shadow that might flicker on the rock in the boy's field of vision. But the boy noticed nothing. He was squatting over his anorak, picking over its contents. Then he moved his head out of the way, and Stéphane saw, spread out on the pale green nylon lining of the anorak, a heap of wheat ears, shrivelled and dry but still full of grain, some nasty looking weeds, a handful of beans and, in pride of place, an egg.

The boy's hand suddenly moved. He had seen the sweets. He picked them up, and whipped his head round, looking back over his shoulder into the cave. Stéphane ducked his head out of sight. The boy was anxious, Stéphane could tell from his rapid movements. He was hunting round the cave, peering into the crevice, going to the entrance and looking up and down the lane.

He came back, and stood upright in the funnel. Stéphane could hear him breathing only a little more than a metre away, and could almost sense the heat of his body. He lay absolutely still, his eyes screwed up tightly as if shutting them would help him remain invisible. If the boy stood on tiptoe, if he jumped a bit to look higher, over the lip of the funnel, Stéphane would certainly be caught. But the boy didn't jump. After a long moment, he ducked back down again into the cave, and Stéphane heard him move sticks around on the fuel pile.

He must be laying the fire, he thought. He'll find the matches in a minute.

He was deeply excited at the thought. He'd never set out to help anyone in secret before. He was filled with a strange, intense warmth. He couldn't bear to keep his head down any longer. He had to see what was going on.

The boy had smoothed the dust away from a bare patch of earth with his hands and was building a tiny wigwam over a nest of dry grass. He was working with total absorption, placing every twig with thought and precision. Then he stood up and looked down at it.

He doesn't want to light it, thought Stéphane, hugging himself. He thinks he's only got one match. He's scared he'll blow it.

The boy was fussing over the food now. He brushed some earth off the beans, cut them into short lengths and put them in the can. Then he spent a long time on the wheat, rubbing off the chaff and picking out the grains, working slowly and deliberately.

He's putting it off, thought Stéphane delightedly.

The boy picked the egg up several times, nearly cracked it on the edge of the tin once, but put it back again. Then, suddenly resolute, he reached for the matchbox and opened it.

Stéphane stuffed the end of his T-shirt into his mouth to stifle the squeak he'd almost let out. He needn't have bothered. The boy's gasp was loud enough to cover more than a squeak. He dropped the matchbox as if it was red hot, and jumped to his feet.

Edgy, thought Stéphane. Suspicious. I would be.

The boy was anxiously hunting round again. Stéphane heard him leave the cave, and waited for him to come back. There was silence for a while, then from the thick undergrowth that ran up the hillside beside the cave came the snap of twigs breaking and the rustle of leaves.

He's coming up here, thought Stéphane, starting up like a hare, and breathing in short, nervous gasps. He won't like me watching him. It'll all go wrong.

Silent and slim, he wormed his way up through the dense bushes, following the winding patches of grass which offered the quietest, easiest passage, working his way up the hill. Within minutes he was in the wood. He paused. He could hear the boy still, above the cave. He was trampling round in Stéphane's own hiding place. He must have seen the beaten grass where Stéphane had been lying. He must have noticed the fresh scrapings in the earthy sides of the top of the funnel where Stéphane had pulled himself up.

It was harder to move quietly in the wood. The leaves rustled at every step and hid dead sticks which would go off like pistol shots if he trod on them. Stéphane edged forward, stopping and listening at every step. He heard the boy go back down to the front of the cave, and the faint metallic sound of feet kicking the loose stones in the lane, just as he reached the wire that separated the wood from the field.

He waited there for a long time, watching the rabbits, noticing the entrances to their burrows for future reference, then his sensitive nostrils caught a whiff of wood smoke.

He's lit it then, he thought, and delightedly punched the air with his right arm.

He toyed with the idea of creeping round to the front of the cave and seeing what he could from there, but rejected it. There was no cover from that side, nowhere to hide at all. Regretfully, he slipped down the hillside keeping to the shade of the trees, back to join his special route home.

It would be supper time soon, in any case. He'd wait until morning, then he'd bring something big, something wonderful for the boy, like a blanket, or some clothes, or a saucepan. With a really big present in his hands he'd find it easier to show himself, and the boy would understand, then, where the sweets and matches had come from. He would know he had a friend.

{31}

The uneasy feeling he'd had that morning came back to Peter as soon as he stepped into the cave after his second foray at the farm. He was tense enough already. He was sure he'd nearly been caught. He'd found a good lot of wheat, as he'd hoped, although at least half the ears that had looked edible at first sight had turned out, on closer inspection, to have been eaten out by mice or birds. Then he'd gone round to the back of the farm again, to the wall which separated the lower edge of the vegetable garden from the field.

There had been no need to go near the farm buildings at all. It would all have been fine, he could have had as many beans, tomatoes (only he was not keen on more of them), cabbages and leeks as he wanted, but he'd been stupid. Lulled by the Sunday afternoon sleepiness, the absence of the hens, who had scattered out into the field, and seeing no sign of the dog, he'd been tempted by the hen-house's open door, had crept in, found an egg almost at once in the straw, picked it up, and was stealing back to the vegetable garden when the stupid dog had got wind of him.

The woman must have been doing her flowers round the front or something. She was round the corner of the house in no time. It was only by a miracle that he was already so near the tall vines of the runner beans, which offered perfect shelter. He even picked a few of them while he waited, hoping she would go away.

Then he heard her anxious voice, much nearer than he had expected.

"Qui est là? C'est toi, mon petit? Viens!"

He'd been terrified that she would take the dog off its chain, and loose it on him at any moment. Perhaps it had been silly to take the risk, but it seemed the only thing to do at the time. He had leaped the garden wall and made off across the open field, knowing she must have seen him, remembering only in his panic to hang on to his egg, his wheat and the beans, and to disguise the direction he was taking, to avoid going straight to the cave.

It had been a huge relief, a real home-coming, to find his bed, his fuel pile and his other stuff exactly as he'd left it. It was only slowly that this odd feeling, this sense of not being quite alone, had crept up on him again.

The sweets had scared him at first, but not for long. People might easily have been here on a Sunday afternoon, while he'd been up at the farm, picnicking the way his family had done. Kids could have dropped the sweets accidentally. He was only glad he'd happened to be out when they had come, and that they hadn't mucked around with his bed.

He made his preparations for supper slowly, aware that it was still quite early in the day for an evening meal. He wasn't looking forward to lighting the fire. His hands felt clammy already with nerves when he thought of that one match, that half of a match that had already failed him once.

He made a sudden decision to put it to the test and get it over with. It would be better to try lighting the fire earlier this time, so that if he failed and wasted the second match, he would have longer to work out other ways of doing it.

He reached for the box and opened it. It was half full of good, unused matches.

His first reaction was horror. He snapped the box shut and jumped to his feet. Someone knew he was here. Someone was watching him. A noose was round the cave. If he made a false move it would tighten round him and trap him.

He'd looked round the cave before, when he'd found the sweets. Now he searched it properly. There was no sign at all of an intruder. He went outside and looked up the hillside. He should have thought of the back entrance, the green funnel, earlier. Perhaps he would find traces there. Quickly, he pushed his way up it.

It was obvious someone had been here, and quite recently too. Peter saw the marks of feet on the soft wall of the funnel, and the outline of a body in the long grass, just by the top of the funnel, It was a small shape. It could only have been made by a child, and quite a small one too. He felt better. A child wouldn't threaten him. He'd only seen one child around here, the boy at the camp site, and he'd been hiding matches then, too.

Slowly, Peter retraced his steps. The matchbox was still on the ground where he'd dropped it. He picked it up and this time, when he opened it, he was flooded with gratitude towards the boy, or whoever had left it there.

He took out a match and struck it. His perfectly built wigwam ignited at once. He fed it with bigger sticks, until he had a good blaze going. It wasn't really too early to start his supper. It was going on for six o'clock. He would take more trouble this time, boil the egg, then cook the rest of the stuff properly, and have time before it got dark to brew up another load of soup, if he wanted to, with the rest of the wheat, and maybe some dandelion leaves or something. Then he would go out and get a good handful of blackberries, and it would be like having a proper pudding.

It wasn't until much later, until he'd eaten his egg, had burnt his tongue a couple of times on the hot mass of beans and chickweed, and scraped out the soggy swollen wheat grains from the bottom of the tin, that he had time to think again. But, as the light slowly faded and the colour ebbed out of the fields and sky, and he drew back into the cave and settled down near his fire, he began to feel anxious again.

They'll get me, he thought. That woman at the farm, she saw me, I know she did. They'll be back to look, like they did this morning.

He shifted his position, and saw, behind his sitting rock, the bright glint of cellophane. He'd hidden the sweets there, saving them for this moment after supper. He unwrapped one, and put it in his mouth.

If that boy had left the matches here, he thought, he probably dropped the sweets, too.

He tried to remember everything he could about the boy, and the people at the camp site.

He is planning to run away, he thought. I'm sure of it. He's stocking up. Bet he wants to use the cave as a hide-out, like me. He probably doesn't even know I'm here.

For a moment, he felt threatened, as if the boy was about to take the cave away from him. Then he remembered the strange feeling of being watched that he'd had before he found the matches.

He does know I'm here, he thought. He was watching me. Why didn't he show himself?

He stood up, suddenly anxious.

He'll tell someone! He'll get them onto me! They might walk right in and catch me when I'm asleep! They might come at any moment, Scarface, or his wife, or the man from the camp site, or the gendarme. They might be creeping up on me now, surrounding the cave, ready to leap in and . . .

He darted over to the front entrance. The lizards had retired for the night, but he could still see their shiny tails lying alongside each other in their favourite crack in the rock. He didn't know why they comforted him so much.

Cautiously, he poked his head out and looked around. The valley was wrapped in a profound twilit peace. The heron was flying with slow, measured wing-beats along the dark line of trees that fringed the stream, its neck folded back into its shoulders. The cows were clustered in a reflective group, their white flanks showing up as milky patches against the dim grey-green grass. A troupe of starlings had settled in one of the oaks near the rabbit warren on the hillside above. He could hear their twittering quarrels as they fussed over their favourite perches.

No other human being was within half a mile, he felt sure of it. He knew in his bones that he was quite alone, and was reassured and felt safe again.

He won't tell, he thought, remembering the wildness in the way the boy had run. He's like me. He's on the outside, only he always has been. He's the real thing.

It was comforting to know that the boy was there, that he had something like a friend in this solitary place.

He went back to his fire. He fetched some good-sized pieces of wood from the fuel pile and placed them on it carefully.

"Don't you dare go out like Sparks did," he said.

The fire laid into the new fuel and crackled noisily. It was a different thing from Sparks, not a friend, not an ally, just a fire. He would be glad of it tonight, and make sure it stayed on, but he wouldn't need it as he had needed Sparks. He wouldn't be afraid of the noises of the night, of bats, or owls, or foxes, or even of the ghostly shadows cast by the moon. He didn't have to give them silly names now in order to drive out his fear.

Other things frightened him tonight. He was scared of people coming for him, trapping him,taking him away. Even more, he was scared of what would happen if they didn't come. He was changing. He was getting used to being alone. He would soon get used to hiding, and stealing, and killing animals.

Maybe, if that boy ran away, and came here, we could do things together, he thought. It wouldn't be so bad then.

For a moment or two, he enjoyed the idea of living in the cave with someone else. He imagined telling the boy about the fish trap, and showing him the spring.

"But I can't speak French," he muttered out loud, "and they'd find two people much faster than one."

It was stupid to think about the boy any longer. He had to think about himself. He had stayed here because he thought Mum and Dad would come back for him. They'd had more than enough time to do the journey two or three times over. Only some terrible disaster could have stopped them. He knew what it was. Mum had given up and gone off. She had left Dad with Billie. They'd all been too wrapped up in themselves to think about him. They might not even have noticed that he was missing. There was no point in thinking about going home. It wouldn't be home anymore, not if Billie was there instead of Mum, and he had to live for ever and ever with Julian.

He had to make a decision. He could stay here, in the cave, and live like an outlaw, keeping out of sight, picking up whatever food he could, making things and managing on his own, at least until the weather turned cold. The alternative was to leave at once, find his way back to the autoroute and get himself somehow to Calais, and across the Channel. He could go and see Dad and tell him – ask him – beg him –

An owl hooted close by. It made him jump, but it didn't frighten him.

It's not animals, it's not the dark I'm afraid of any more, he thought.

He'd made up his mind. He would leave in the morning, early, before it got too hot. He would find the autoroute in the end, if he just kept trying, he was sure of it. He would go home, and speak his mind. He would force them to listen. He would make them listen.

He built up the fire, slipped his anorak on and lay down, his head on the pillow of moss. The bed wasn't comfortable exactly, but it was bearable, much better than the hard rock of the night before. A bat flitted close by over his head.

"You can shove off, the lot of you," said Peter, and shut his eyes.

{32}

Madame Favier slept badly. She didn't usually wake until Roland, sitting up in the high, old-fashioned bed beside her, set the ancient springs creaking and groaning as he swung his legs over the side and groped for his trousers. But this morning it was different. She'd lain awake for hours, waiting for the crack of sky between the half-closed shutters to lighten, and for the blackbird to start off the dawn chorus from its high point in the wild cherry by the barn.

Poor little boy, she thought. Poor little boy.

Tears had rolled out of the corners of her eyes and into the iron grey curls over her ears. Visions of the English boy, hungry, frightened and exhausted merged and mingled with another child. She still fancied sometimes that he was nearby, outside in the dark, shivering and hungry, and she would cry because she couldn't help him. Roland would look anxious, and say something clumsy and rough to comfort her, and it would make her cry even more.

Madame Favier got up as usual before the sun rose. It was always a mistake to talk to Roland first thing in the morning. He liked to get out of the house and off to his milking with no fuss and bother. He would never offer more than a grunt until he'd come back in and taken his first gulp of hot coffee and a bite of breakfast.

She heard the door handle below rattle and the plastic fronds clatter as he went outside, then she got out of bed herself. In the night she'd made all kinds of plans, to go out and search on her own, to look in the unlikely places, by the quarry, in the derelict mill below the château, in the woods above the cave, but now she was up and the day had started, she was caught once more in her usual round of chores.

She'd finished feeding the hens and was in the kitchen putting Roland's coffee on when Katie started barking. Madame Favier lowered the gas and went to the door. Chassot was outside with another, older gendarme, and a stranger, a tall, blond man in crumpled jeans and a sweat-stained shirt who looked as if he hadn't slept or shaved for days.

"Bonjour, Madame." Chassot looked as fresh as paint, his moustached face as bright and cheerful as the stranger's was haggard and distraught. "This is Monsieur Castle, the boy's father."

Madame Favier was flustered. She'd built the father up in her mind as an ogre, a selfish, careless brute. She'd imagined finding the boy by herself, taking him in, protecting him against his casually wicked foreign parents. Now she saw the wretched man's face, and everything changed. He was the suffering soul at the centre of this drama. She was merely an onlooker. She heaved a sigh.

"Ah, Monsieur . . ."

Chassot could barely suppress his excitement. The

entire region was being ransacked for this English child. Radio and TV stations were broadcasting appeals and descriptions. The major at Moulins, even the colonel at Vichy, were taking a personal interest in the case, and it was in this very district, in St Didier-des-Bois, that the breakthrough seemed likely to come. The father, who had set off with Mercier from the Moulins headquarters before dawn, had recognised something at last – the outline of the château with its two round donjons, from the road.

Chassot saw in his mind's eye a triumphant discovery, the child restored to his grateful father, a TV interview, a congratulatory clasp on the shoulder from the brigade major, promotion . . . He refused to think of the alternative – the inert bundle of limbs in some foul, hidden corner, the grisly business of the medical and forensic units, the covered stretcher, the sickening hunt for the killer. The boy would be found alive and well here, this morning, he felt sure.

Madame Favier was babbling something, trying to get out the words.

"I told you, yesterday. The way he ran! My vegetables, my eggs, well, and my cheese as a matter of fact, over the wall. You remember, don't you?"

Chassot shot an uneasy look at Mercier. He felt on his mettle with this older man from headquarters. Perhaps he should have taken Madame Favier more seriously yesterday, followed it up . . . Fortunately, Madam Favier's speech was too garbled for the others to follow.

"Yes, of course, Madame. That is why we have come straight to you," he said hurriedly.

"He's in the cave, I'm absolutely sure of it," said Madame Favier, surprising even herself with her own conviction,

"And Monsieur Favier is . . .?"

"Not back from the milking. But wait –" she was stripping off her apron, and ran inside to put it down. "I'll come with you. Take the car right up to the cave and you'll scare him, poor little . . . He can run very fast, you know. And frightened? He must be terrified. Well, you would be. Imagine, in a foreign country! And men in uniform, too. Now, my shoes, just here, under the chair . . ."

Peter woke twice in the night, disturbed by marauding insects the first time and a screeching night bird a few hours later, but he was so utterly exhausted that he fell asleep again quickly, untroubled by the wild fears and fancies of the night before. Some sixth sense must have been on guard, however, because in his sleep he heard low voices some way away, which stopped abruptly after a louder "Sshh!"

He was up and in a crouching position at once, every sense alert. He'd slept much later than he'd intended. The sun was well up already. The fog of sleep rolled away instantly, and his mind was racing.

They're here. They've come for me. The noose. The trap. Get away. Find the autoroute. Escape.

The sound had come from the lane, in the direction of the camp site. If he went out by the front and ran the other way they would be sure to see him. He could run fast, but not for long, and they knew the country better than he did. He'd never get away.

He looked wildly round the cave. For a moment he thought of the crevice, imagined himself hidden in there, crammed into the corner, out of sight unless they searched really hard, but then he heard running footsteps crunching in the lane. They were almost on him.

Some instinct from deep inside leapt up and took control. Before he fully realized what he was doing he had gone for the green funnel and was clawing his way up it with frantic scrabblings of his hands and feet. Then he was out at the top and bent double, zigzagging up along the grassy patches through the undergrowth as Stéphane had done the day before.

He reached the barbed wire that edged the wood, slithered under it and stopped. He felt safe enough for the moment to pause and take stock.

Cautiously he edged his way to a vantage point where the trees met the field. Someone was just disappearing into the cave, and the woman from the farm was running in after him. And outside, standing still and looking up slowly and searchingly at this very hillside, were two gendarmes.

Peter's heart was thudding painfully, and there was a singing sensation in his ears. He looked round frantically for a way of escape. If he came out of the wood on either side he would be on the open slopes above the lane. He would be seen at once. He would have to go on to the top of the hill and try to get over to the other side. He'd never been over the hill before. He would be in completely strange country. But there was no other way out.

He bent low again, hugging the ground like a hunting fox, and began to run as silently as he could, choosing the barest ground between the close growing trees, towards the top of the hill.

Mr Castle recognised the cave from a good way off, and would have broken at once into a trot to get there faster if Mercier had not put out a restraining hand.

"Slow, my friend," he had said in his thickly accented English. "He hear us, he is afraid, he run away."

"Sshh!" Madame Favier said irritably, placing her feet with care on the grass verge.

Mr Castle contained himself for a few yards more, then burst away from them, careless of the noise, ran the last two hundred metres and plunged inside the cave, his hopes raised to fever pitch. He saw the bed, the still smoking fire, the empty egg shell and the sooty tin can, then he pounced on something that was lying on the ground.

"His knife!" he said, in a squeaky voice. "He's here! Peter! Where are you? Come out, Peter! It's me! Dad!"

It took him a while to realize that the cave was empty.

Trembling with disappointment, he joined the gendarmes outside, leaving Madame Favier to wring her hands over Peter's disintegrated bed.

The gendarmes were standing stiff and still, scanning the hills, like greyhounds trying to pick up a scent.

"His knife," said Mr Castle, holding it out to Mercier. "He's here. Hurry! Hurry! Please!"

He wanted to act, to run somewhere, to chase Peter. The gendarmes ignored him.

"He'll have gone out of the back entrance and up through the wood," said Mercier quietly. He turned to Madame Favier. "How far does the wood extend? Can he get out at the top?"

She shook her head doubtfully.

"There's a very thick hedge and a lot of wire reinforcement. It's the boundary of our land. My husband renewed it last year. I don't think even a little boy could force his way . . ."

"Look!" Chassot had grabbed Mercier's arm. "Up there! On the right!"

The thin, tense figure of a boy had wriggled out of the wood through the wire into the field at its highest, narrowest corner. He was trotting jerkily along the hedge, hunting for a place to get through.

"Run along the lane and cut him off," barked Mercier to Chassot. "I'll go up the field after him."

Chassot hesitated, watching the boy. The hedge at the far end of the field arced down to join the lane. Mercier was probably right. Unless the boy found a way through higher up, he would have to come down and get out through the gate at the bottom.

The boy had seen Mercier now. He paused for a moment, in anguished indecision, casting round for a way out, like a wild animal frightened for its life. Then he made a decision and began to leap down the hill to the gate at the bottom.

Chassot took off, sprinting like a thoroughbred.

He can't see me, he thought. The hedge is too high. He reckons he'll outrun Mercier, but I'll catch him at the gate.

But Peter got to the gate first. He slithered round the gap behind the gate post, and without a backward look began to race away down the lane. Chassot swore. Then he heard another, heavier pair of feet pounding up behind him.

"Peter! Peter! Stop! It's me! It's Dad!"

Peter swerved violently and slowed for a moment, as if he'd been hit by a bullet. He seemed to trip, to be about to fall headlong, but he righted himself and without a backward glance, raced on.

"Peter! Come back! Peter!"

Chassot slowed as Mr Castle overtook him. He saw the boy falter again, and the big man catch up with him. He saw Mr Castle's arm shoot out and catch Peter's shoulder, and he heard Mr Castle's howl of pain as Peter sank his teeth into his father's hand.

He watched as the fight went out of them both, and they stood looking at each other, then he ran up, afraid that the boy would bolt again.

"It's all right," said Mr Castle very gently. He put his arm round Peter's shoulders, and tried to draw him into an embrace, but Peter stood rigid, staring straight ahead, refusing to look into his father's face.

{33}

Peter hadn't said a word since they'd picked him up in the lane. He'd sat stiffly in the back of the gendarmes' car, between Madame Favier and his father, and had looked straight ahead at the two gendarmes' heads, not answering Mr Castle's increasingly tentative questions.

"Where to now?" Chassot said jubilantly. He felt good all the way down to his boots. It was for moments like these that he loved his job. Only a tinge of anxiety was clouding his joyful triumph at being the instrument of this father's happiness. He had hesitated down there in the lane a moment too long. The boy had almost got away. Had Mercier noticed? It was important now to do everything correctly by the book.

"Back to the farm," said Mercier. "Didn't you leave a message for the mayor to meet you there? I thought you said he was an old teacher. He'll probably be able to speak English. Anyway, he's the proper person to take a minor into care."

Chassot looked round at him in astonishment, and nearly missed the turning up to the farm.

"What do you mean, into care? The father . . ."

Mercier shrugged.

"The kid doesn't look too happy to me. Might be a case of abuse or something. We'd better keep an eye on him when he gets out of the car. He looks all set to bolt again."

Monsieur Gérard's fastidiously polished Citroën was already drawn up outside the farmhouse. Chassot parked alongside it, and both gendarmes jumped out quickly, each one unostentatiously covering one of the rear doors of the car. As Mr Castle got out, Chassot noticed for the first time how strange he looked. He was not radiant at all, as one would expect a man to be, when his lost child had been miraculously restored to him, but visibly upset. He stood helplessly while Peter nipped out of the car after him, not knowing what to do or say.

"Get them inside, quickly," Mercier muttered. The boy was looking round sharply and nervously as if he might take off at any second.

Madame Favier eased herself out of the back seat with difficulty, and broke in on the tense silence with a rush of words. She had been mentally scanning her larder during the short journey home, and was fired with hospitable enthusiasm.

"Not enough bread, I don't suppose, it being Monday," she said, her thoughts spilling over into speech without regard for her listeners, "but at least there's plenty of ham and that good Brie from yesterday. Poor child, so thin, of course they don't feed them properly, do they?"

She was oblivious of the watchful silence of the three men and the boy. Her feelings got the better of her. She swooped suddenly on Peter and pressed him against her large soft breasts, then, still with an arm tightly round his shoulders, propelled him towards the door of the house and in through the plastic fronds.

Chassot and Mercier exchanged sheepish grins, then a yellow barking streak suddenly shot round the corner of the house and launched itself at Mercier's trousers. He backed away.

"Shut up, Katie! Get down!" shouted Chassot. To Mercier's surprise the dog dropped onto its haunches at once, and panted up expectantly at Chassot.

"Thank you, my friend," said Mercier with feeling, and Chassot, his confidence somewhat restored, led the way into the house.

Peter was frozen up inside with anxiety, and his brain, jolted so suddenly out of sleep, was twisting and turning in confusion. His worst fear was coming true. He'd been caught by the police and now they'd brought him to the farm to confront Scarface, who was sitting at the table arguing with a rotund little man, waving a hideous knife in the air. And Dad had said nothing about what was really going on. Dad was against him, like the rest of them.

Everyone was talking. They looked uneasy, and kept glancing at him and Dad as if they were waiting for something to happen. Only the woman was ignoring them. She was clucking round like one of her own demented hens, setting out plates and cups, unwrapping pieces of cheese from their waxed paper covers, and cutting thick slices off a vast round loaf of bread. The gendarmes were standing by the door, almost as if they expected him to make a dash for it, as he had thought of doing when they'd arrived at the farm.

His eyes were getting used to the gloom after the dazzling early morning sun outside. No one seemed to be taking much notice of him, no one except Dad, who was standing beside him in a state of dreadful, empty stillness.

He doesn't dare tell me, thought Peter, in a sudden rush of fury.

"I'm not going to live in the same house with Julian," he said very loudly. "You can't make me."

At the sound of his voice, the two men at the table and the gendarmes by the door fell silent, and Madame Favier, approaching the table with a full coffee pot in her hand, stopped where she was.

The worry lines on Mr Castle's forehead deepened even further. What dreadful things could have happened to Peter in the last forty-eight hours? How could he have changed, in only two days, from a normal, chatty boy to this silent, withdrawn stranger? Had he become deranged?

"What do you mean? What's all this got to do with Julian?" he said, thoroughly bewildered.

"I'll run away if you do. I can manage on my own. I've done it. I don't need you any more."

A spasm passed over Mr Castle's face. Monsieur Favier dug Monsieur Gérard in the ribs and turned up the fingers of one hand in a gesture of enquiry.

"What's he saying?" he hissed.

Monsieur Gérard held up his own hand in a dignified request for silence. His English, nevermore than rudimentary, was rusty with decades of neglect. He could understand a few words but couldn't pick up the gist. He saw no reason to explain that to Roland.

Mr Castle tried to take hold of Peter's elbow.

"Peter, I don't know what you're talking about. Are you all right? Has someone attacked you, or hurt you? Did you . . ."

Peter shook his hand off.

"Yes, you do. You know what I'm talking about. You and that woman. Where is she, anyway? In the car? I won't go back to England with her. I'd rather go to prison here."

"What woman?" Mr Castle was beginning to understand, but wasn't ready to admit it.

Peter could hardly bring himself to say her name, but when he'd said it once, he found he could not stop.

"Billie!" he shouted. "Billie! Billie! Billie!"

"Peter," Mr Castle was choosing his words carefully. "Did you think that Billie was . . . that I . . ."

"You're going off with her, aren't you? You're going to divorce Mum and marry her."

"What is this 'billie'?" whispered Monsieur Favier loudly.

Monsieur Gérard raised his eyes to heaven.

"Chut!" he said severely.

Mr Castle pulled out one of the chairs from the table, and sat down heavily.

"Peter," he began, then shut his eyes. "My God, Peter, it didn't even occur to me that you'd notice – I mean that you kids – you all seemed quite happy."

"Come off it, Dad. You're going to, aren't you?"

"No!" Mr Castle almost shouted. Everyone jumped, and Madame Favier, suddenly realizing how heavy the coffee pot was, put it down on the table. "Of course I'm not leaving Mum. I'm not going off with Billie, or anyone else for that matter."

The five fascinated watchers saw the thin boy in his torn, filthy clothes relax for the first time. Peter awash with relief, felt as if he'd been flying in the dark out of control and had picked up the lights of the landing strip ahead. Then he saw the look on his father's face, the strain and sadness, and it was as if he was seeing everything, Dad, Mum, Billie, home, for the first time in his life. He recognised, in a flash of understanding, Dad's patience with Mum's nerves, his silence when she nagged at him. He thought of Billie's good nature and her kindness, the ice creams she'd paid for, the casual friendships she'd struck up wherever they'd gone. He thought of how Dad had been happy with Billie, had laughed and joked, and been careless and comfortable and easy.

"I'm sorry, Dad," he mumbled.

Mr Castle shook his head in disbelief.

"You're sorry? You're sorry? Good Lord, Peter, you've

got no idea, you can't imagine – these last two days – I was afraid you were dead. I've been torturing myself. It was all my fault. I know it was. I can't bear to think . . ."

"It's okay. Really."

Mr Castle put his hand over his eyes. Peter knew he was crying.

"Knock it off, Dad," he said, filled with embarrassment.

Mr Castle suddenly grabbed Peter and pulled him into a fierce hug. Madame Favier let out a great sigh and wiped the corners of her eyes with her apron. Chassot swallowed a lump in his throat.

Mercier was unaffected.

"That's it, then," he said to Chassot. "It's looking good. You'd better go out to the car and contact your chief. Tell him he can call off the search and inform the press. The kid's been found safe and well and restored to his father."

Monsieur Favier pounded frantically on his friend's arm.

"Well? Well?" he demanded. "Are you going to tell me what's going on, or have you been conning us all these years with your wonderful knowledge of English?"

Monsieur Gérard smiled at him indulgently.

"Calm yourself, Roland. You have just witnessed a beautiful scene of reconciliation. The son asked forgiveness of the father, I can't think why. The father asked forgiveness of the son. They have become fully reunited." He saw more questions forming on his friend's lips, and turned hastily to touch Mr Castle on the arm.

"Mister Castle," he said, bringing out the words he had been rehearsing in his mind for the last five minutes with a flourish that impressed Monsieur Favier as much as it infuriated him, "we are all very happy that you find your son. Please accept our felicitations. You are a father. I am a father. I understand your joy. I participate in it."

Mr Castle took a handkerchief out of his pocket and loudly blew his nose.

"Thank you very much, all of you," he said, looking round the room as if he was becoming aware of the onlookers for the first time. "You have been very, very kind."

"Ask him if he wants some coffee," said Madame Favier, hovering anxiously over the cups," and the little one – milk? Bread? Ham? Make him eat something!"

Mr Castle understood, turned and smiled at her.

"Merci, Madame," he said, and patted the chair beside him.

"Breakfast, eh, Peter?" He turned back to Monsieur Favier and struggled to find the words in French. "You have a telephone, Monsieur? I'll pay, of course, but please, I would like to call my wife."

{34}

It was the most wonderful breakfast of Peter's life. He came back from trying to cope with Mum's tearful questions on the big black telephone in the corner of the room to a bowlful of warm milk with a dash of coffee in it, slices of ham, yellow, strong-tasting, crumbling butter from Madame Favier's own churn, wedges of soft cheese melting with ripeness and a plateful of small, sweet, green plums.

The only thing he didn't dare to try, or even look at, was a goat's cheese, still on a twin of the saucer he had taken from the cheese cage behind the farm.

Everything seemed fine. Everyone was full of kindness, loading him with questions, but he didn't feel safe. Even though Scarface, when you came to look at him close to, was not as frightening as he'd seemed – had quite kind eyes in fact – he was still threatening, with his hunched shoulders and powerful forearms. And the gendarmes were still there. The older one had pulled a chair up to the table at once, and was cutting large bites off a pale pink slab of pâté. The younger one, who had gone out to his car, had come back chuckling, and had accepted a cup of coffee from Madame Favier with a broad grin. It looked as though everything was all right, but he couldn't be absolutely sure. Not yet.

"What did you do? How did you manage? Did you find anything to eat?" Dad was looking at him hungrily and bursting with awkward questions.

"I stayed in the cave, most of the time."

That was safe. There was nothing wrong with that.

Chassot spoke rapidly to Monsieur Gérard who nodded and cleared his throat, as though he was having to force the English words through a fine clogged mesh.

"Peter – your story – we all wish to hear. After, you go to the – to the gendarmerie." He saw the wary look return to Peter's face and smiled at him reassuringly. After thirty-five years in a village classroom, he knew boys. He knew that look. This one, he could see, was a little difficult, a bit of a challenge. He was the unpredictable, the sensitive type who could turn either way, scared of authority, prone to feel guilty, but likely to surprise you. This boy would require a little tactful management. To be tactful in English – that was the challenge.

"There is no problem, Peter," he said slowly, watching the boy's face. "The gendarmes of the brigade want – wish-want to meet you only. To shake your hand. They worked for you, to find you, you know? And Monsieur Chassot –" he slapped the younger gendarme on the knee "– he says the journals, the television, the whole media, they arrive at St Didier, they want your story! Voyons, Peter, you are a celebrity!"

He was rewarded with a dazed smile and a further loosening of the skin around Peter's taut eyes. The boy was worried about some little peccadillo, some minor transgression, that was clear. Monsieur Gérard thought rapidly.

"To eat – to live – one must eat, quand même! – perhaps a few vegetables from a garden, a little cheese, a fish from the stream, it is not a crime. My friend here –" he turned and punched Monsieur Favier lightly in the chest "– my friend is happy if you eat his tomatoes!"

Monsieur Favier jumped.

"Maurice. if you don't tell me what's going on, I swear it, I'll . . ."

"Relax! I told him what a generous, big-hearted . . ."

"It's true," said Madame Favier, with another gusty sigh.

". . . old softie you are. I told him he was welcome to all your tomatoes, your trout, your wife's cheeses . . ."

"Hein?" Monsieur Favier was scowling, the scar on the side of his face drawing his lip back into a truly ferocious snarl. Monsieur Gérard saw Peter stiffen up again.

"Look what you've done, terrified the boy again, just when I'd got him ready to talk. Take that look off your ugly mug or he'll bolt again."

Monsieur Favier growled and held out his bowl for Madame Favier to replenish. He sounded so like a cantankerous old dog that everyone burst out laughing.

"Ah, mon petit," said Madame Favier, her round cheeks pink with enthusiasm, "you could have had all my cheeses! When I think how you have suffered . . ."

Peter, though he did not understand, saw that she was

on the point of coming round the table to embrace him again, and he hastily plunged his face back into his milky coffee.

"Now," said Monsieur Gérard, judging skilfully that the moment was ripe. "Tell us, Peter, slowly and clearly, how you eat, how you sleep, how you do everything. La France entière waits for your story."

A wonderful feeling of well-being was creeping over Peter. It was like waking up and finding that the every-day, safe world was still there after a terrible nightmare. The reality of the past few days and nights was still clutching at him, but it was becoming weaker as each moment passed. This beaming old man, who somehow reminded him of his first head teacher at his primary school, seemed in some uncanny way to know all about the cheese, the vegetables and the fish, and he had actually hinted that it did not matter. The gendarmes seemed equally unconcerned. Far from gazing sternly at him, as the instruments of cold justice might be expected to do, they were politely thanking Madame Favier for their breakfast and waiting eagerly for him to begin his story. And Dad – Dad was the best of all. He'd come back. He'd suffered agonies of remorse. He'd not gone off with Billie and rejected Mum. Peter felt better about Dad than he'd ever felt in his life before.

He put a final plum in his mouth, though he was feeling so full he wan't even sure if he'd be able to swallow it, and spat out the stone.

"Well," he said happily, "I was okay. I stayed in the

cave. I made a fire."

"How?" Dad was admiring.

"I tried it with two sticks, but it didn't work. I got blisters. He held out his palms, saw how filthy they were and, full of embarrassment, quickly sat on them. Everyone laughed. Encouraged, Peter went on.

"I found some matches. There was – someone, at the camp site. I saw . . ." he hesitated. He didn't want to talk about the boy hiding the matches. It would have been a betrayal. The boy hadn't given him away. Peter would keep his secrets, too. He hurried on. "I found a tin can and a water bottle. There was a spring with good water."

Monsieur Gérard was attempting a simultaneous translation, but the word for matches escaped him. It was just as well, for, at the mention of the camp site, Monsieur Favier's growl had rumbled again.

"I made soup in the can with nettles and stuff."

Mr Castle was shaking his head in disbelief.

"And I – caught a couple of fish."

"But you didn't have the rods! They were in the car!"

"I made a trap."

Peter was anxiously watching Monsieur Favier's face as Monsieur Gérard translated this information. To his relief, the farmer nodded and the ghost of a smile flickered round his leathery lips.

"It was very well made, very clever," he said. "Thank God we don't have English poachers in France."

Monsieur Gérard translated the first part of this response, but tactfully suppressed the second.

"I caught two fish," said Peter proudly. "I cooked them on a grill made from a bit of old wire, like in my survival book. I can't tell you about it here. Can't we go down to the cave, Dad? I want to show you everything, the lizards, and the spring, and everything."

There was a rapid exchange of questions and answers in French.

"Why not?" said Mercier. "It's on the way back to the gendarmerie, isn't it?"

"More or less," said Chassot doubtfully.

"And if there's really going to be a press conference, we must give the boy time to make a full psychological adjustment before we expose him to the media. You know what they're like."

"Of course," said Chassot, who had no idea.

"Quite right." Monsieur Gérard got to his feet and flicked the crumbs from his linen jacket."I'm coming with you."

"It's all right for some," grumbled Monsieur Favier, going to the hook by the door from which the keys of the tractor were hanging. "I've got work to do."

He came up to Mr Castle and shook him vigorously by the hand.

"Au revoir, Monsieur," he said. "You've got a fine boy there. Pity he can't speak French, that's all. Glad you've found him safe and well, but make sure you teach him not to nick other people's vegetables in future."

Mr Castle smiled uncomprehendingly and pumped Monsieur Favier's hand in return.

"Merci, merci beaucoup." His French was inadequate to express the strength of his feeling. "Attendez, un moment."

He felt in his pocket, took out his wallet, pulled out a card, and gave it to Monsieur Favier.

"My address. If ever you come to England, come and stay with us," he said. "Vacances. Chez nous. En Angleterre."

"A holiday? In England? When does a farmer ever get the time to go on holiday?" said Monsieur Favier derisively, but he gave the card to his wife and told her to put it on the mantelpiece where important communications of an official nature were kept.

"Merci, Monsieur," said Peter, blushing fiery red with embarrassment at finding himself actually speaking in French. "Et pardon – er – pour les tomates et le fromage."

Monsieur Favier let out a crack of laughter and patted Peter's shoulder with a heavy hand while his wife approached dangerously near. Chassot was holding back the plastic fronds. Peter ducked through them, followed by Mr Castle and Monsieur Gérard, and dived into the car. From the safety of the back seat he waved at her enthusiastically.

"Merci, Madame! Au revoir!" he shouted, as the car speeded up down the lane.

{35}

Stéphane had lain awake late constructing plans for helping the English boy. He'd thought of taking him some bedding – a pillow, or at least a blanket, but after sweltering all night in the stuffy trailer he'd decided against the blanket. It would be useless in this weather. The pillow wasn't such a good idea either. It was too big to smuggle out of the caravan easily, and would be missed at once. Anyway, Peter had made a good enough one of his own out of moss.

"Pétaire," said Stéphane to himself, practising the unfamiliar English name. He'd heard it last night on the TV news. There had been an appeal by the police, and the father had been on – all the usual stuff. Stéphane's parents hadn't even lifted their eyes to the TV screen, but he'd been transfixed, especially by the photograph. He'd been able to take a good long look at the boy for the first time, front view, face on.

They'll get him soon, he thought with regret. They'll get the dogs on him.

He had gone to sleep so late he woke up long after he had planned to. He raised his head and looked over at his parent's bed at the far end of the trailer. Monsieur and Madame Bourlaud were still stretched out on their crumpled sheets, dead asleep. Stéphane, moving with practised efficiency through the cramped space, slid into his clothes, eased open the door of the food cupboard and made a swift selection. A hunk of bread, a chocolate bar, a packet of biscuits and an end of garlic sausage were all he could manage to carry. He hesitated over extracting a plastic carrier bag from his mother's basket, but decided against it. The rustle would be bound to wake her.

He ran silently and quickly to the cave, keeping to his special route, wormed his way up to the top of the green funnel through the undergrowth, and lay down on his patch of grass, waiting for the effect of any sound he might have made to wear off before he dared lift his head and look down into the cave.

He knew at once that it was empty.

He waited for a long time, hoping he'd made a mistake, then he gathered up his presents and slipped back through the bushes to the lane. With infinite caution he inched up to the mouth of the cave and looked inside. The boy had gone.

He's probably up at the farm, getting more of that goat's cheese, he told himself, but he knew in his heart of hearts that they had already got him.

"Stupid git," he said savagely, raising spurts of grit and dust as he kicked at the stones in the lane. "Softy. "I wouldn't have let them get me. I'd have hid myself roperly."

He was sick with disappointment. He was sick with

himself. If he'd only woken earlier and got here when he'd planned to, he might have helped Peter. Two always worked out better than one. He could have been a decoy. He would have let himself be caught even.

In the dead silence of the early morning he picked up the sound of the gendarmes' car, starting up at the farm over half a mile away. He hid the food in the ditch and retreated out of sight, back into the undergrowth. He hesitated at his usual place on the patch of grass, but as the car came into view and he saw the blue lamp cone on the top, he decided it would be safer to get further away, and he went on up into the wood.

Peter had wanted to show Dad everything, his fire, his bed, his pile of fuel, his cans, but the moment he stepped into the cave with his father while the two gendarmes waited in the lane outside, his feelings changed. Everything looked smaller and somehow insignificant. The bed was only a heap of dead grass, the fire just a few cold ashes, the can a piece of sooty junk.

"You know the dam Rachel and Sophie did, in the stream? That's where I made my fish trap," he said, wanting to get Dad out of the cave again. "It was great. It really worked. I wish you could have seen it."

"So do I," said Dad.

He looked choked up again, as the bleakness of the cave brought back the full strength of his remorse.

"It's a great cave," said Peter anxiously. "You should have seen it when I had my fire going, and I was cooking my supper."

Mr Castle nodded, speechless. Peter hurriedly picked up his can.

"Look, I made the handle out of wire. It was the first time I ever really used the spike on my knife."

Mr Castle took the knife out of his pocket and handed it to him.

"Here it is," he said. "I found it here. That's how I knew you were still around."

Peter opened out the spike.

"See, Dad? It's good, isn't it?"

Mr Castle scarcely looked at it.

"You actually slept here? You weren't scared?"

"Not last night, really. The first night, I was. Scared stiff. Terrified. There were dancing shadows and noises and stuff like that."

"What did you do? I mean, how did you . . .?"

"I just – I don't know . . ."

Peter looked round, seeing it all through his father's eyes. He didn't want to talk about it, any of it, any more.

He went back to the mouth of the cave. The lizards, disturbed by the movement and voices, had flicked themselves into a crack in the rock. Peter automatically put his knife down on the sitting boulder, in the little hollow where he had kept it always to hand these past two days, in the place where it had seemed to belong. He parted the grass gently.

"Look, Dad. Lizards."

"Oh, yeah." Mr Castle did not bother to bend down

and look at them. He seemed unable to take his eyes off the pile of dead grass.

"Monsieur Cassle!" Chassot was calling from the lane. "Vous êtes prêts?"

"They want us to go," said Mr Castle. "Have you shown me everything?"

"Yes," said Peter. He waited until his father had gone, then he took one last, long look round the cave, and at the two glittering bodies, nestling in their crevice.

"Goodbye, Robert. Goodbye, Stripey."

A beady eye glinted back at him, wary and expressionless. Peter picked up his anorak. He'd forgotten the knife.

Suddenly he thought of the boy.

"Good luck," he whispered.

As soon as the car had turned the corner and was out of sight, Stéphane ran to the edge of the wood and boldly out into the open field. There was no point in hiding now. He'd seen the boy being taken off by the police.

The rest of the summer stretched bleakly ahead, friendless and pointless.

He might still make a dash for it, thought Stéphane hopefully. He might come back. I'll look after his stuff for him in case.

It was strange to approach the cave openly, as if he owned the place. He stepped inside and looked round, enjoying the coolness and the wafts of fresh, earth-smelling air after the heat beating down outside.

I could take it over, he thought. Sort it out a bit. Do a fire, and cook stuff myself.

Then he saw the knife.

He watched it for a moment, almost afraid it would move and disappear of its own accord. Then he suddenly snatched it up. It fitted his hand perfectly, as he had known it would, as the boy must have known it would.

He did see me, then, thought Stéphane. He knew it was me gave him the matches. He left it for me.

He could already hear what Mum would say, when he brought the knife out in an offhand way at lunch time.

"Where'd you get that then? Nicked it, didn't you? You'll go the same way as your brother, you will. Don't say I didn't warn you."

And he wouldn't answer for a moment, just look down at it as if he'd had it for a long time, and say very casually, "No, I never nicked it. It was a present. A present from a friend."

Elizabeth Laird – Author Profile

Elizabeth Laird was born in New Zealand in 1943 but she grew up in London. She has lived in many parts of the world, including Ethiopia, Malaysia, Iraq and Lebanon. She has a special interst in Ethiopia, where she once taught, and where she has travelled widely, collecting folk stories. She now lives in London with her husband, David McDowall, who is also a writer. They divide their time between London and Edinburgh.

Elizabeth Laird has won many awards, and has been shortlisted four times for the Carnegie Medal. Some of her books are set in Britain, but some are set in the Middle East and Africa. Her work has been translated into more than fifteen languages.

For more information, visit her website at elizabethlaird.co.uk

Another Barn Owl book you might enjoy

THE SILVER CROWN

Robert O'Brien

£5.99 ISBN 1-903015-08-1

This powerful and magical adventure begins when Ellen receives a mysterious crown for her birthday. Bravely facing the tragic and sudden loss of her family, she sets out to find her way to her much loved Aunt Sarah. But who are the sinister men in green and why do they seem to be hunting her down? At Ellen's every turn lies danger and mystery but with the help of her friend Otto, she determines to uncover and fight the evil. After all, Ellen *is* a Queen . . .